T0106177

ADVENTURES

in my beloved

MEDIEVAL ALANIA

and beyond

A TIME-TRAVEL NOVEL
SET IN THE 10TH CENTURY
CAUCASUS MOUNTAINS

Anne Hart

ASJA Press
iUniverse, Inc.
New York   Bloomington

ADVENTURES IN MY BELOVED
MEDIEVAL ALANIA AND BEYOND
A Time-Travel Novel Set in the 10th Century Caucasus Mountains

ASJA Press
an imprint of iUniverse, Inc.

iUniverse books may be ordered through booksellers or by contacting:

iUniverse
1663 Liberty Drive
Bloomington, IN 47403
www.iuniverse.com
1-800-Authors (1-800-288-4677)

ISBN: 978-1-4401-1955-2 (pbk)

Printed in the United States of America

iUniverse rev. date: 1/27/09

Contents

CHAPTER ONE

Arrival

Princess Raziet-Serakh's Tale: Queen of the Steppes

Mount Elbrus: The Year 865 of the Common Era

Dear Diary: This is Raziet of Alania and Karachay-Balkaria who is now called Serakh of Khazaria:

My life adventure is resilience and to find a voice that resonates all of my confidence. Now in my youth just before I will become sixteen years of age, my confidence speaks all about lighting a wonderful brightness and walking out of the darkness of insatiable banalities. With the renewal of spring, the world is repaired, and the gardens bloom in my magnificent Alania. I walk up steep hills and ride far to remember each intimate glimpse of blooms on trees and to listen as waterfalls whisper. We have come up here all the way from Sarkel to remain here in the mountains, close to my childhood home.

To insure my confidence, my voice, and my resilience, here I light the eternal flame to brighten the damp room. I am Raziet, now called Serakh. I am Karachaian-Balkarian, and from my grandfathers, of sweet Alania. I am partly Khazar and partly from the peoples that dwell by Mount Elbrus. I am all of them, all mixed together for generations. My many ancestors came from Persia, the Kavkaz, the Steppes, and beyond where the sky rides the moon.

I am the tamga of the horse, the orchards, my pet wolf, and the open grasslands. And today, I am here, not where the Volga meets the Caspian, but with our friends and my cousin breathing deeply the sparkling air beneath my Mount Elbrus. We wait in our aoul. We are all of my magnificient Alania, and here now, in this land of orchards to the north, the scent of the birch trees, the patina, the starlight, my venture, value, and vision. Sit at my table and experience the eternal light of Khazaria and the rest of these mountains and rivers from the Caucasus to the seas of Pontus and Meotis. We are all one from many in the joy of life.

And suddenly the gift of one pair of Tabriz sleeve-sitting cats arrived with the silk and saffron. Still I'm not going to marry the Emperor of Byzantium on my sixteenth birthday after all. Instead, today, my father, the Kagan of Khazaria, our spiritual leader and King, who adopted me from Alania when I was so young, my father, has lit the Sabbath oil lamps and walked out of the darkness.

The Kagan may have thought about it for years, but in my fifteen-and-a-half-years-old eyes, it seemed as if the few families of our court of Khazaria turned Jewish in the time it takes water to make a grain of wheat sprout. I wonder what my friends and cousins in Alania, and the Karachay and the Balkarians with whom my ancestors intermarried, each with their different languages, will be thinking about the *joy of choice* now that I've finally settled just north of Alania, in Khazaria. Listen, dear diary, *it's all about the joy of choice.*

Oh, the joy of *choice* about whether to become Greek or Jew or wife of the new Caliph of Baghdad or Pagan in the world of nature, or to place my tamga, the one with the white horse, as a charm, under my pillows for good luck. On the other hand, there are always the steppes, my Caucasus, the mountains of my grandfather, and eastwards of my mother, my cousin's Urals, or the Altai of their wives. And then, there are the horses to care for with acts of kindness.

And I listen to the songs of the Silk Road all the way to the feasts of fragrant Persia of my mother's ancestors. But here I am in the Caucasus by Mount Elbrus that is my uncle's homeland, and soon back in my beloved Alania, just south of the Kagan's empire, Khazaria, surrounded by the isinglass boats that go up and down the Volga between Kazan and the Caspian, the Khazar Sea, also called in our times, the Sea of Meotis.

These times we have to tend our orchards if we want to eat. That means settling. With *this many horses*, how can we settle?

Now, what am I supposed to do next? Write a song? And so I did that to the tune of my 86-stringed kanoun that came here all the way from Mosul. And I played my song while my brother accompanied me on his four-stringed lute, a present from a Kazakh.

"I'm not going to shave my head and wear two braided tresses at each temple," my youngest brother, Marót insisted with an attitude. I placed my new cats on my lap and groomed them.

"Father says you have to." I whispered.

"No."

"You'll look like a great Khazar warrior. Look, the Bek wears his hair that way already."

"Not my long hair."

"Yes, your hair."

The Bek is supposed to run his armies, lead the country, and command his Tarkhan. Yet today, my nightingales of the Caspian, he took my thirteen-year-old brother, Marót, shaved his head, and left two thick waist-length dark brown braids on each side of his head at the temples that look like columns that frame his green-gold eyes that remind me of autumn colors—leaves and ochre.

Then the Bek, our administrator, put his small daughter in my care and told me to teach her how to pray over the Sabbath lamps on Friday evenings. Who's going to teach me? Everything changed so fast, that I found myself dancing with my three-year old cousin. I even had to change my name. I'll name my cats after myself.

Don't Khazar girls have names? It seems as if nobody records them. You'll remember mine, Raziet-Serakh, light of the Caucasus, Alania, and the Crimea. It's Hebrew and given to me long ago by the dutiful wife of rabbi Ha-Sangari of Byzantium when I time-traveled to past centuries. My name used to be Raziet, nightingale of the

Caucasus, Alania and Khazaria. I am a Khazar, but before my family joined the Khazari, I was born from a grandfather who is Karachaian-Balkarian. I am a child of Alania, and also a child of both Khazari and Karachay peoples of the Caucasus and other ancestors from the steppes of the great horse breeding cultures. I am a child of everywhere and of these orchards.

This year my royal Khazari family and also my family of Alania, and my mother's family from both Persia and Ossetia and many more in my lands turned Jewish. Yes, we were only a few from Alania. My first task that time began by introducing Kasher cooking to the Queen of the Steppes whose name changed after the fourth century of our common era.

I brought forth the queen into this time from six hundred years in our past. She still mixes her yogurt with lamb like the Romans of generations before us that she dwelled among. Maybe it's because today's Caliph of Baghdad has his laham b'adjin roasted that way with the yogurt gravy basted over the top as the lamb turns on the spit.

Taklamakan, the Queen of the Steppes, makes her own rules about what foods may be mixed at the same meal. Silk had a civilizing effect on Taklamakan.

Taklamakan must have told me a hundred times that long ago, when Alaric, a Goth, besieged Rome, his price for sparing the city included 5,000 pounds of gold, 3,000 pounds of pepper, 30,000 pounds of silver and 4,000 tunics of silk. And her price, four hundred summers later, is double that number of tunics of silk from our Khazari royal family and double that number of Khazar-minted silver yarmaq coins.

"Impossible," the Khatun would say. "We are a small nation."

"No you are not," the Queen of the Steppes answered. "You are an empire that spans the mountains between the two seas, including the shores of the Dnieper and Volga Rivers unto the camps of the Pechenegs. And I want my silver and silk before the Kievan Rus drive you north of the great mountains."

"Are you sure that six hundred years ago we were allies of the Tribes?" the Kagan would ask their leaders.

"With friends like us, who needs the Pechenegs?" They would assure my father.

One time the Byzantine Emperor asked the Pechenegs to attack the Seljuk Turks.

"Attack the...who?" The Pecheneg leader shrieked.

"That particular tribe of Turks is both numerous and fierce. We won't attack them. I hope you would be so tactful as to never mention the matter again."

So not all tribes riding out of Central Asia are the same, even thought they may speak related languages. I know almost every word that was said between the Byzantine Emperor and our peoples, and even what is supposed to be our enemies.

Word spreads here like the dry summer fires from the Kafkas to far away Atil and Sarkel.

This summer the Rus princes attacked Constantinople. Emperor Michael III and the main field army dawdled on the eastern frontier, my father told everyone in our court. This left the Rus to destroy the unprotected suburbs on both shores of the Bosphoros.

Well, well, well! Rus from Kiev took the Byzantines by surprise. Mother said the people panicked. She studied their culture well and watched how in the Hagia Sophia the patriarch Photios preached two sermons. All he demanded was that his people repent of their sins to avert the "Wrath of their Lord." Mother's cousin was there.

I'm supposed to be married of soon to a Greek of Byzantium who will ask me to convert to yet another faith. What shall I do? You tell me.

Word flew back to Khazaria that the people marched around their walls with the Virgin's Robes, and other most holy relics from their own religion. The Khatun told our family that a huge crowd chanted their litany and pleaded for deliverance. The worse happened, and I'm afraid it's going to be blamed on the Khazari people. Of course we were not there with the Rus. Those same Rus also attack us and try to do the same here. That's why we built our fortress in Sarkel.

We don't pillage and steal booty from other peoples just because their religion is different. Khazari protect oppressed Jews in their own lands and help them to come to Khazaria if they must leave their homes. I'm a time traveler, and I know everything changes even though it always stays the same.

I know Khazaria will be sacked by the Rus, and I'll be living in another place, but that's a hundred summers from now. So what I'll do then can be put on the waiting list. For now, my father is worried that when the Rus sailed away, they stole an enormous booty from the Byzantines.

Some of that booty is showing up for trade where the Volga meets the Caspian, in our territory. And it's being siphoned off on the Pechenegs, who peck at our borders and make war with us, because they have no way of feeding their children in the place they come from.

I understand when hunger brings new people to a place where there is no room for them and war breaks out over who will feed and who will starve. But this Rus game that comes from the wealthy Kievan princes—to attack us and others, simply because they like to fight.

This, I don't understand, except to say perhaps they need more work to do or more learning to enjoy. Everyone seems to be fighting the Pechenegs. When will someone reach out and help them? The Kagan still fights battles with them.

Why doesn't someone ask them what they need to be happy and how they can also have full bellies and a sturdy roof for their children? Is there not room any longer already—for all of us? They should time travel with me and the whole family, and see how much room there is in this world when we spin into the future. So now it's the Pechenegs.

Oh, the Pechenegs and their encampment of war wagons with high wooden sides that let them fly their arrows through the holes made in the wood. If we find them, they become our chicken coops. Sometimes the Pechenegs live in their war wagons and don't bother to put up those nomadic tents and yurts!

They're supposed to be the enemy, but I don't believe in enemies. I have a Pecheneg little friend. He's an orphan, and I actually adopted him. The Khatun had to know what she was doing when she let me adopt a five-year-old Pecheneg orphan. I couldn't let him stand there, alone. So now he's my little brother.

The Khatun told me that The Pechenegs are gaining control and that we Khazari are slowly losing control over the central Asian steppes. What are we doing there? Our homeland actually is near Derbend in the northeastern Kafkas. We came up here. But our first homeland was in Atil where the Volga flows into the Caspian Sea.

Anyway, the Pechenegs took advantage, moving west through our Khazar territory to occupy the Rus steppes in an area stretching from the Crimea to the Caspian Sea. From this new homeland, the Pechenegs began to fight with their neighbors, and that includes us. The Pechenegs fought with the Khazari and Ghuzz in the east and the Magyars and Bulgars to the west.

Fortunate for them, they positioned themselves number one across the Varangian trade route to Constantinople. Why only last month the Pechenegs raided Rus and Byzantium. You'd think they would stay enemies, but no, money called.

When not raiding, the Pechenegs hired themselves out to the Byzantines as mercenaries.

So that explains why I go around with a five-year-old Pecheneg boy most of the time as my little friend and brother. No, people don't always have to be enemies just because the Bek has an argument.

I found this little boy, named Togrul, the tenth, after the Turkic mythical hawk, with a Pecheneg chieftain who carried papers telling of the Pechenegs new alliance with Tsar Simeon of the Bulgars. Simeon hired the Pechenegs as mercenaries to assist him in driving the Magyars toward the west.

Meanwhile, Simeon and his Pecheneg mercenaries forced the Byzantine Empire to pay a humiliating annual tribute. Still, amidst all that business, one orphan boy caught my eye, and I told the Khatun. A five-year-old boy shouldn't be wandering the battle campsites looking for something to eat.

Pecheneg, Bulgar, or Byzantine, an orphan is an orphan. So I gave him a home with me and my family. He'll be reared as a Khazar, with me in charge of his early indoor tutoring and my older brothers asked to teach him the outdoor arts.

A Pecheneg woman took him from the Pecheneg Chieftain. He was a cute little boy, well fed and stocky with olive skin and long black hair.

Togrul wore his hair like his big brothers in battle—braided into a pigtail that he stuffed under his cap exactly like his big brothers stuffed their pigtails under their war helmets. Khatun took off the little boy's cap and heavy war helmet someone had given him, probably belonging to his father after he became an orphan.

We gave him a present—itakh, puppies. The Pechenegs dressed much like we Khazari, men and women wear. Our brown felt boots, blue trousers, a long black under-tunic split at the front for riding, a forest green caftan, a short gold overtunic and a brown cloak. As people moved away from the line closest to our Kagan, the fabric woven turned from silk, and brocade to wool, fur, and linen, or leather.

Of course, in Atil, the winters required fur, wool, or leather over the wool and fur. And the colors and fur trim with reams of embroidery depended upon the status and wealth of the person.

In winter, all our cloaks looked the same—fur or thick wool. Our felt or wool caps are trimmed with fur. And the armor is for the men and boys—scale, chain maile, lemellar, leather, and quilted fabrics.

All the women make the quilted fabrics. That's what women wear in the cold weather, quilted tunics under the cloaks, and in brighter colors. As a girl, I don't carry a shield, but my brothers do. Their shields are made of wood and leather or they are osiers.

Why they carry small, circular shields I don't know. They won't carry the heavy tortoise shields so they could assume the turtle formation like the Romans did. No, they have to carry the light weight small, circles.

The Pechenegs tie whips around their arms instead of using spurs. They dress like us, but maybe their small shields won't help them much.

It's not easy to tell a Pecheneg from a Khazar. Perhaps their hair is blacker and ours are browner, or their olive skin is but a shade deeper than our sallow peach complexions. In battle, we still look almost the same, Central Asian mixed Eurasian faces that could vary from the reddest of redheads to the most Asian looking among both of our tribes.

We are made up of many different people from many different places, and really, nobody thinks it's important if someone's hair is black, red, or brown. The little Pecheneg boy I carried away to be now part of my family and a brother wore the studded leather caftan of his father in battle, a brother of a chieftain. His mother trimmed his cloak in fur around his wrists just like on his uncle's cloak, with brocade along the waist.

Like his Pecheneg uncle, the boy carried a spear, no shield, and wore a helmet with chain maile and a piece of metal for his nose protection. His uncle wore a rounded Pecheneg helmet with metal protection from his cheeks up to his eyes.

Someone cut holes in the metals so he could peer out and see, and the rest of the helmet had chain maile protection for his lower face. Our Khazari helmets are sometimes pointy and solid above the ears.

There is a solid metal face mask on our own helmets with chain maile protection for each man's ears and neck. One of my cousins makes these helmets and showed me all the different ones when he spoke with me about all the tribes in our part of the world.

So the little orphan boy stays with me now and calls me sister. No matter how fiercely the Pechenegs fought the Khazari, I'm sure the little boy's mother (wherever she floats now) is glad that I am taking care of her only child.

He now lives with the royal family of her deepest enemy, a Khazar princess, and most preciously, a Judaic family, but I still put a little amulet of his father's favorite horse worshipped by this Pecheneg tribe, under his bedclothes. His uncle trusted me with it.

Amazing, since the Pechenegs had lost a battle to the Khazari, and his whole family disappeared. No, we didn't massacre his family. They abandoned him, which no one could understand. Pechenegs don't walk away from their children. Someone had captured the wife, but it wasn't the Khazari.

His uncle had put the child in our care because he was ill from drinking bad water. He had made peace with the Byzantines, but wanted this boy to be raised by the Kagan of the Khazari. I don't know why. Someday I will ask his wife who is not a Pecheneg, but comes from another tribe who lives in the central part of the Kafkas just north of the Adigye.

Today is the day that the caliphate of Harun ar-Rashid ended, says my time-traveling father. Long live the new regime and rose petals to bless his people and the peoples of this Earth, known in the far past and far south as Eridu. Say it fast—

Eridu—and it sounds like Earth. My father and the Bek accepted the faith for themselves and our families. Father asked the people to choose their faith. The first to follow, Alp, the Brave, our cousin, known as Alp Tarkhan, commander of the Khazar armies, lit the oil lamps and walked out of the dark. Since the Kagan and the Bek had the same Turkic name, father took the Hebrew name, Zachariah, and the Bek remained, Bulan. I mean, how many men named Bulan, the elk, can you have in one royal court?

Yet father at first wanted his name after his favorite Kagan, Busir Glavan, who ruled a hundred winters ago when the great Yehuda Ha-Levi came here to give us a first glimpse of what would be our destiny. And the rebellious Bek, more warrior than worrier, insisted on the name, Xan-Tuvan Dyggvi, after the Kagan who rebelled. That event took place thirty harvests past.

Father took the Hebrew name, Zachariah, because the traveling Ha-Levi made an impression on his grandfather so long ago. Levi's precious gifts fired from his eyes. He meant the scrolls, parchments, letters, and books to be read and shared.

Then there were my brothers, Marót, the youngest, then Awchi, the hunter, Barsbeg, the panther prince, our helper, Bolushchi, Khatir Il-

Teber, the strong builder of fortresses, Tarmach, the translator, and even the keeper of all our dogs and wolves, Kasar. Everyone lit the oil for the festival of lights, but not the Queen of the Steppes who lives on her side of the river. Everyone thinks she's part of the Magyar migration, but she stands alone in her own fourth century world in our ninth century golden age.

She always says, "You stay on your side, and I'll stay on mine." Now, why would a Queen I time-traveled out of the fourth century listen to a Khazari girl born hundreds of years in her future?

Rain almost never came to her side of the river. And before I could say "khatun" without sneezing, wouldn't you know it? She camped on our doorstep. She visited us, perhaps because I'm next in line to be the Khatun of the Khazari. Or maybe she came here because I hold the key to the Caspian, the Sea of Khazari. The Queen of the Steppes came to our fortress, asking for one of my nine brothers-as a husband. I guess loneliness drove her here.

Here I was stuck for the hot, dry summer in Atil, near the smaller river called Atil, where the delta of the bigger, Volga River pours into the sea. I'm so happy we left to travel several days' journey, riding into the high Caucasus. Actually we took our time and spent almost a full moon to full moon cycle riding slowly up here.

You won't find me hunting the wild boar of the steppes anymore. Even my brother stopped, and he's now touring the Yeshivot he's building like the ones he saw in Persia.

We don't eat boar nowadays. And since the lambs and goats over grazed the place, the steppes are turning brown. So we moved here for the cool breezes of Mount Kazbek. I'm afraid now that I'm a prisoner of the mountains I think even more of my home in Astrakhan and the Crimea.

Days are musical and filled with learning from my tutors who are the wives of the Persian rabbis in our town of Atil, in this Hebrew year of 4620 that is the year 860, according to Byzantine missionaries Cyril and Methodius who arrived at my father's court.

There's my father, the Kagan of Khazaria. That's right, the one with the long, drooping dark mustache. He's the one who appointed the great rabbi Ha-Sangari of Byzantium to convert us Khazari to the Judaic faith and law. And right in front of the missionaries sent by the rulers in Byzantium.

Sssh, don't tell, but the Kagan still sleeps with the tamga, an amulet of a white horse under his bed clothes for extra luck and a parchment of Torah scroll in his mezuzah that he had placed on the door for a blessing. In Hebrew that mezuzah signals a mitzvah.

That's a new word now for me, my favorite word--mitzvah. It not only means a commandment and a blessing, but also I like the word, tzedekhah, or charity. I must learn how charity multiplies.

Next to my father, there sits the Bek, Bulan. He rules with my father, but the Bek takes charge of the business at hand and the armies. My father, the Kagan, is more like our spiritual leader and the one who brings everyone together under one roof.

It is as if the whole Khazaria was the same family from many different places. Khazaria is a miniature model of the world. I mean we all have to live here together, even though we may have come from different places long ago.

I have a lot to learn from the Persians and those who fled Baghdad who also are fleeing into our homeland. In the past two years, long before we actually all took the Judaic faith here today at the royal court, I learned to read and write in Hebrew from my tutor who has sung the Baghdadi rite.

My father calls me his "golden flower of the steppes." I'm Princess Raziet-Serakhof Balanjar, a Khazari, and daughter of the great Kagan and tutored in the fine art of poetry. Now I also use my Hebrew name to carry along with my Turkic name. I'm not only called Raziet-Serakh, but Shoshanna, which means "rose flower" in Hebrew. I'm afraid I'm more than a flower. My name is what tea the Khatun sips—'rose' blossom water with cardamom, cinnamon, and pepper from the great rabbis of Baghdad.

Because I was raised with the Queen of the Steppes, the Kievans in the north lands also call me and her Khatun, Queen of the Steppes. Yet we come from different places. I was born in Himri, a village in the district of Arrakan, in the north-west part of what you call Daghestan, and I was reared in Atil.

The Queen of the Steppes says she is an Altai noble from the western deserts of Mongolia. Our main city, Atil lies close to the Caspian in this corner of the mountains. Our summer house is near the sea, the Sulak, just above the point where the main stream throws off one of its four branches which is termed the Andian Koissu, and the mountains run in a single arc between the Caspian Sea, the Sea of the Khazari, on my left and the Sea of Pontus, near Byzantium on my right.

My mother is the Khatun, Queen of the Khazari. She already has taken a Hebrew name, Amyra. We, like others from our ancient homeland near Derbend use the title, 'Khatun' for our queens. Mother, who came from Persia, is a tiny woman with large tree bark-hued sloe-eyes and hennaed hair that shines like burnished copper. She is used to seeing houses of worship that face south and honey cakes that point toward the north star.

Her hands and feet are like a child's. She always carries silver lace, honeysuckle or jasmine, and washes in bitter orange blossoms boiled and rinsed through her hair that reaches to her waist. We Khazari wear our hair pleated in braids and doubled in back.

Our winter hideaway isn't in our main cities of Atil or Sarkel, but in the mountains of the Caucasus. This stone house here in Himri is dustyrose in color, overlooking a small hill where the rivers meet.

The land I call home forms the two sides of a triangle of mountains, having for its base the high Caucasus that we call the Kafkas or the Vladikavkaz. The apex of the mountain is just below Himri, and consists of the cliffs of two summits called the Touss-Tau and the Sala-Tau.

When I look up at the mountains, it is almost as if the cliffs are escaping their lacey bonds to be free, like the glutton's fleshy belly spilling over his belt. Himri, together with the neighboring village of Akhulgo, is one of the keys of this triangular region of well-watered highlands. Only as long as I can remember, the rains haven't visited here.

One hot, dry summer turned into a colder and dryer winter. The famine in the East is bringing torrents of refugees into our lands full of rats and fleas. No one knows to bring out the cats. I've brought mine out—my Persian kittens, all clean and shiny with bushy tails.

Who lives here besides the Khazari? Many different tribes walk these hills and valleys of apple orchards. This is our original homeland, and now other war-like tribes dwell here. They are known as the Lesghi. We have the territory of Dagestan we call Derbend in the east Kafkas or Caucasus Mountains to visitors. And other tribes have the land of Chechnya on the north. We move between Himri and Atil, where I live with my parents, the entire royal family, and of course, my daring 13-year old brother, Marót.

Our house is like an eagle's nest high on a rock projecting from the mountain side. From the beautiful vale through which winds the Koissu, the Kagan ordered a narrow path cut out of rock.

His men carried stones zigzagging up to a height of two or three hundred feet. There, the path downhill was exposed to be swept by stones let loose from above on any enemy that might be daring enough to look about the fair beauty of his only daughter, me Raziet-Serakhalso known as Shoshanna, or approach his youngest son, Marót, my brother who is just over a year younger than I am.

The Bek, our Kaganate's administrator, built a triple wall supported by high towers to add to the defense of our fortress that we call home. Who do we wish to keep out? Not the Silk Road tribes, for we have been their allies for the past six hundred years.

Who then? The Rus of Kiev? The Byzantines? The Viking long ships trading on our rivers whose widows we marry when they tell us they want to choose our faith? The new Caliphate to our south and east? Who will surprise us this year? Are we the only people offering choice?

I'd rather not be at my needlework, the sun glistening in my henna-rinsed, dark auburn braids. More often, I'd be swiftly galloping my new mares and racing my brother, Marót.

For five years now I saddled my own solidly built white gelding, slipped my bare foot into the stirrup, and rode into the dawn. Here I go again, talking of the freedom of the steppe when I'm as sheltered as my house by the overhanging brow of the mountain. Each day I stand on one of these towers and look down upon the narrow but fertile valley, divided in two by the fast-flowing river.

I watch and wait, like all women, wait for my destiny to arrive-until one day I decided to take my destiny by myself like the Queen of the Steppes across the river. It was something about the surrounding mountains laid out in terraced gardens, partially covered with oaks that set me free as a Khwarizm Kazak with a tymakh. Bet you can't say that tongue twister without asking what's a tymakh? You wear it.

My mother, the Khatun, Queen of the Khazari, a tiny speck in the distance came slowly forward, swaying against the drapery of foliage under the gold and purple tines which the rising sun shed over the ruggedness of the limestone. Then I rode to her on my white gelding from a great height clad in white like the perpetual snows. I rode down the winding path, westward where the view is stopped short by the white shroud of Mt. Kazbek.

The sound of the waterfalls reminded me of the Bek, the administrator of our lands and the commander of the armies. He rules over the Tarkhan, the commander who barks at the warriors like my pet wolf, Kasar. Bulan keeps a summer hideaway near the great waterfalls.

My mother brought flower-water to wash her husband's feet because that is what queens must do as they learn to understand charity. She mingled fearlessly amid the groups, kissing the hands of strangers before seating herself on the divan. She had yielded her cheek, without a blush, to the lips of her children.

A lot happened in our world since the Kagan turned those who wished in my whole country to the Judaic faith today. Ahmad founded the Samanid rule in Transoxiana last summer, the Bek told me. This summer, someone murdered the Abbasid Caliph Mutawakkil Muntasir. Hasan b'Zaid established the Zaidi state in Tabaristan. Woe to the rooster who is setting up the Khazar armies. Father pours over his Torah and isn't aware yet of who pecks the Bek and who scratches at the Tarkhan, but for what? My brothers have told me the fortress has ears.

What need of these facts would I have if I weren't to be someone's queen? I don't want to be Queen of the Khazari someday. I want to care for my animals. It would probably be worse to be the Queen of another land. I won't marry the Byzantine Emperor, for I just converted to the Jewish faith, and I can't now marry into the Steppes.

That leaves me little choice. Perhaps I can leave that decision until next year. Whatever I decide, nothing will stop my thirst for writing poetry. Wouldn't you have guessed it?

Just when I start learning to write well, someone has burned down our most important library. And if I go off to Baghdad, I'll run smack into a flood of Jews fleeing that city for Khazaria. So it's our duty to go to the aid of the oppressed. Perhaps there's land for me to the West. Scholars from Spain come here.

Luckily, I have more freedom than anyone I know. And I still can ride my gelding so high into the mountains that no one would come looking for me. I'd be perched in an eagle's nest. From there, on a clear day, I can see the world turning over.

"Khatun," the Kagan called, sipping his thick, sweet tea. "Khatun, Marót should be in school studying so he can become a learned healer. At this rate, he will never be able to study Torah with the great rabbis who are coming into our lands."

Our streets are steep and crooked. Only Khazar roofs are flat. Our walls are almost without windows. Even the palace is built with unhewn stones to be rough.

Our house lies half-buried under the rocky mountain side. To be a Khazar is to be settled with orchards, but in the nomad's way in houses without torah scrolls, streets without names.

It would be easy to wipe out a people so unrecorded in reality. No village spire points up. No sundials mark the hours. There are no Roman water clocks. Who cares about time here? What difference could a day make? Before the conversion, time was unheeded, except for morning, noon and evening.

We have had houses of prayer here since people who pray came to this land from everyplace along the Silk Road, let alone the steppes and all from corners of Europe and Asia. And now the Persians build their houses of prayer here with windows facing west, and the Kievans build their houses of worship with the windows facing south.

Each has his own place facing a different direction, according to the custom from where he came. What they all have in common is the white stone and the wood of the birch trees. You'd have to look at the windows to tell them apart.

In a dark corner illumined by aslant rays from a small high window of yellow-stained glass, a rabbi from Baghdad speaks to another from Prague. They have a third language in common. From dusk until dawn not a light is seen throughout the village. We have mountain men here who call our village their aoul. They teach us their Zikr dance by jumping over a stick held shoulder high leaping back and forth.

When the dance stops, scarcely a sound is heard. My watch-dogs yelp and the jackals cry in the forests. Only at noon does life appear in the streets. The women tend to their gardens. The children play games such as throw the bones to the jackals. Little boys learn to shoot arrows from the age of five. They drink down their yogurt with a little honey and rose water and lop the head off a bull or a heel of cheese by the age of twelve.

The men sit about idle. Some lie sleeping or stand grouped together in long, pastel trousers. They clean their weapons and groom their houses. Once in a while a wagon covered in leather is seen. A few women come and go. European and Mongol side by side. Nobody makes a distinction.

The children in varying degrees of one or the other are everywhere. Wherever nomads came from to settle here and plant their orchards, they are all now part of this rainbow Kaganate. Most women are in their kitchens wrapping sheep's milk cheese with thin pastry dough. They make our fine Khazar silver lace. The young children, half naked, play around the doors and in the lanes, noisy in contrast to the adult tone of grave repose.

For Marót, one of my nine brothers who's a year-and-a-half younger than me in age, he spent half the day in riding and archery practice when the Kagan wanted him to sit with the tutor he had brought from Baghdad and learn mathematics.

"I heard my name," Marót said, as he walked toward me. "Who are you talking to?"

"My diary," I answered. "I was about to write that you excel in the art of persuasion."

"I'm spending too many of my days with my head stuck in the corner," he laughed. "And all my nights are wasted watching the horses."

"I think you're too young at thirteen to see your first battlefield," I told my brother.

"Would you rather have me spend my next twelve years at the house of my school-master training to be a Khazar warrior?"

"Well, no," I said. "Father has judged you a man."

"Am I not disciplined enough for you in the manly exercises and war arts?"

"Not until the pageant when you're restored to your father," I insisted. And the event begins tonight.

Both of us arrived for the feast ahead of all my father's relatives. The Khatun included Marót's school-master, his atalik, who is a mountain man, not a Khazar. The school-master is from the land closest to the peak of Mount Elbrus.

Marót's tutor returned to our summer house loaded with presents. It is a proud day for Marót. His atalik told him in his own language of the mountains that now my brother is a full-man, a deli-kan.

"For the past two years I wondered how I could prove this to father?" Marót shouted with such eagerness that his school-master had to hold his ears.

"The wars are not yet over," I told my brother.

"Have you ever thought of learning a few more languages?" I cheerfully suggested. I still think thirteen is too young for the battlefield."

"What would you rather have me do for the next year?" Marót scowled at me over his shoulder in a voice dark as lava. Leave it to my youngest brother to grow into a Khazar with an attitude instead of a moustache.

"I'd rather you prepare for your conversion."

Marót twisted his mouth. "I already have one mother, Raziet-Serakh, dear sister."

"I have to look after the horses."

And with that, I joined the feast. Marót loves his horses. When he's not far away in Atil, he's up here with me in the distant Caucasus. He spends days swimming in the torrent on his horse, dashing at full speed up steeps and down precipices. To aim an arrow, while galloping on horseback, in an instant whipping around his bow from behind his back, and as quickly returning it to place. To hang deliciously suspended from the side of the horse so as to avoid the aim or game of an enemy.

He learned and practiced how to spring to the ground for the purpose of picking up something, and again vault into the saddle without halting. Marót would take aim with such precision as to hit the tiniest and inconveniently placed target while riding at full speed. Only most of the time, it was I, Raziet-Serakh, who would win Marót in riding or target practice. He said I was his equal. This he learned from those around him.

"Marót, come here. I'll never press you into learning like I was pressed, like I was made a

Kagan and a teacher against my will. What will you become if you don't want to go to school like the Jews in Persia and Baghdad?"

My brother turned halfway through the front door. The back door led to the wilderness, the half-wild horses roaming the vista, the front door led to narrow streets and dusty mazes of pastel houses winding crazily into nowhere.

"I won't be a poet, a man hung on days out of place, a man living in the bubble of this village. I'll not be torn into a world I wasn't born for like you were. So leave me alone, father." Marót twisted his mouth.

"The boy should be learning Torah, not be grooming horses. Who wants to be a Kagan nowadays with the war on and?" Father cut himself off and stumbled from the doorway, disappearing into the, apex of the cobblestone street. Mother, the Khatun, laughed and I sat in front of a mirror in a corner and brushed my hickory tresses with a sweet, sickly smile on my face.

"The evil eye on you for staring at yourself in the silver standard," Marót screamed at me as he ran out of the house.

"That boy," Khatun sighed. "I know what he wants from this life, to work little and earn well."

"It is not a question of working little or much," the Kagan laughed. "You are a workingman if you are the next Kagan. To live well you have to sell your country or trade the silver yarmaq far up the river. There's no other way in these times."

"These times, these times. These times are no different than times before. What do you keep harping on 'these times'? War was always with us. So what's so different now?"

"War time is work time." the Kagan answered.

I told them both I was tired sitting in the garden. "You're a woman. What else are girls for? When your babies come, there will be no time even for sleep. Aren't you glad our women marry so young to have such strength?" Mother scowled over her shoulder.

"I'm empty, a prisoner of the mountains here. I would be better off down in the flat, dry plain of Atil or in Sarkel. My whole world is like that. The top of Mount Kazbek is not beautiful, just empty and boiled out. I want something different." I told them.

"Women belong in the home tending their babies." The Khatun said.

"Let her do as she wishes," the Kagan added.

"I don't have any babies."

"You'll have in a few years."

"And what if I choose not to?"

"There are always orphans around after a war.

No one's forcing you into marriage. I'm only trying to make you see how you can help others," said the Kagan. Make tzedekah, make charity. You have no children, fine, but there are the orphans. Start taking them in. No innocent child is the enemy in war. Charity, charity is what you are about as a princess of the Khazari.

He was right about charity and rearing orphans. We had the orchards and could feed them all and knit them warm cloaks. I took some bowls to the large granite table in the middle of the garden. Marót was around the pastures subduing a half-wild horse.

This subduing of a half-wild horse in the herd which is allowed during a portion of the year to roam in the woods and hills, is also a feat practiced by us Khazar cavaliers for the sake of securing the animal. For Marót it was my thirteen-year brother's exercise in horsemanship.

Marót and his friend, Tuvan, of the same age rode into the midst of the herd armed with lassos. My brother selected one of the wildest of the stallions--and secured him by throwing the noose over the horse's head.

He rode widely and sprung upon the back of the animal to make trial of his skill. The horse with its nostrils and dilated eyes exhibited a pitiful glance. There was a contest between boy and horse. The frightened brute sped furiously like an arrow over the hills.

The horse turned and doubled, halted suddenly. It rolled on the ground, crawled on its belly, dashed into the midst of the herd and tried in all possible ways to get rid of the burden he had no fancy for. However, Marót, intrepid, self-possessed, alert sat on the horse's back as if a part of the animal.

My brother waved his hand in triumph after every struggle terminated in his favor. And there Marót continued to sit and hold the mastery until the strong steed, finally exhausted by his efforts, covered with foam with broken spirits acknowledged the superiority of its antagonist.

The animal became faithful to Marót, and was his companion on all excursions. He drank cinnamon tea with him the waters which flowed through the plains of the enemy. He shared with him the dangers of the arrow, and neighed in the hurrah of the onset.

Marót had trained his half-wild stallion to creep after his master like a dog, and lie crouching at his feet in silence. He rode well with his mountain friends. They loved him, all the peoples, and the different tribes speaking their different dialects.

No unkind word was spoken to the house thereafter, nor was he ever beaten. His attachment was one of fury and fidelity until he would in old age be clipped at the mane and tail like a war-wracked king and be turned out to pastures to graze the steppes.

Across the pastures in the hut I worked with the servants, because that's what the Khatun said a princess needed to work side by side with the others. We glided by one another nobly, two women under one roof at opposite ends of a pole.

"To marry in war time is to sow among salted earth." I pouted. "On this frontier it's better each man and woman to stand alone. There can no longer be families"

"Your father is wrapped up in seclusion devoting himself to his beloved Torah and poetry and plants," said the Khatun. "The Kagan is a spiritual man. He wants his work to be in everything that makes the world fresher-smelling and doesn't change with people and wars."

"What we need is a writing system of our own. We are using the Hebrew, but what can we use in trade? People never change much, only weapons change. There always have been wars," I told mother.

"So what?" The Khatun said, shrugging. "There will always be people writing the common languge. And we will always be Khazari, wherever we live and under any other name or any alphabet. We belong where we came from, up here in the Caucasus with the other tribes, not down in the flat plain of Atil where the river stinks of too much trade and too frequent taxes."

#

CHAPTER TWO

──────── † ────────

My Mountaineer Friends

Dear Diary:

I'm back again because the Khatun, my mother, had her newest summer place built at Derbend, in Daghestan far away from Atil and Sarkel and my Khazaria. She built a residence somewhat superior in style to the houses generally seen in the eastern Caucasus. And now, she has sent us to our other house far away in the Caucasus, close to my beloved Mount Elbrus.

Because of its splendor and open ceilings so the sunshine would come beaming in, the prince of Kiev is envious, and he sails his Viking allies in their longboats down the Volga. His eye is turned to take the summer place for his mother,

Olga back in Kiev, where we sometimes visit for the great markets.

We are far from there now, but people meet in Kiev from all along the Silk Road. It's a crossroads of trade and languages, and you'll find everything and anything in Kiev, even a smiling husband with flashing eyes of every hue. We have seen Novgorod and Kiev and many cities.

But our house near Mount Elbrus is surrounded by a double row of strong palisades with a filling of small stones and earth, and is approached through a single gateway guarded by sentinels. Near this, on the inner side, stands a tower for defense, irregular in shape and made of stone. It is not as huge as our white fortress at Sarkel, but the colors contrasted and could be seen from afar: a white fortress for the red Kaganate.

Beyond is the principal building in the village inhabited by the many peoples of the North Caucasus—an Imam and his harem of four wives--one Adyghe, a Chechen, a Cherkess-Karachay, and one Balkarian, all under twenty five years of age. Some of the people are still nature healers.

This would be what I could face if my father chose one faith over the other—wife of the Byzantine Emperor, or the fourth wife to the new Caliph of Bagdad, or what I am destined for along this Silk Road. The Imam's harem across the river, beyond the Pagan Queen of the Steppes, housed a palace of his of wives still young enough to dress their lap-sitting Persian cats in brocade and flowing robes, turbans, and lamb's wool hats in winter. But what I want is my eagle's nest.

The builders smear clay on the sides of the stone the house in which I stay. The two-storied building has a stairway outside leading to the chambers with a verandah on one side and a balcony on the other.

Khatun sits at dusk on a high point of rock where she could survey the vale below and the fantastic summits which towered above it. There my still youthful mother of thirty-one seasons gazes at the red snows under the declining rays. I sit with her and watch the rocks glow in the purple clouds until the valley and the glens were dark. We enjoy seeing the westward snow- clad peaks burning brightly at the top of Mount Elbrus. Over there in the distance is Mount Kazbek.

Light fanned out as the lower mountains faded on sight. Only the heavens and the highest peaks were bathed in the mild night light. We watched as legion after legion of one army or another marched from the borders of their lands.

This was enchanted ground for Khazari and their allies of my glorious Alania, and many other peoples of the North Caucasus, and the tribes of the steppes. The soldiers carried their herbs and blueberries, their goat-skin water bags, and everything they owned on their backs. I watched the Pechenegs from the northern borders meet the Bulgars and Burtas on the plains of the Adyghe and other peoples from the lands to meet at our summer palace of stone, plaster, and timber.

Even the Bek spent his summer at our winter palace. Mother built her dwelling on one side of the loftiest mountains by Himri. Her eagle's nest was carved from the rock. There, the mountain leans and is perfectly desolate. Mother builds her palace in a place in which the spirits dance at night.

In the dead of night strange fires are lighted on this dancing flood of the souls, which reflect on all the mountain sides a lurid glare. Then a great white eagle shakes the air, sighing in the night wind, howling of the coming bands of more people, and still more. They move like a tempest.

The flock is haunted. Where Khatun had her palace carved, no one dares to tread by this rock after sunset. It was precisely here that the Queen of the Khazari selected her throne. This place was so far from Atil, the core of Khazaria, that no one would come up here but the local tribes. To stay alive, isolation meant freedom. Trade meant war.

Yet we needed the books and scrolls, and all the wisdom of the world.

Transfers and changes always came from the city. What came from the mountain were the traders who had been to Persia and brought me the thick, clay-like henna that the Arab and Persian women use to tint their dark tresses the russet auburn shade of autumn leaves. Here, far from Khazaria, in this bird's nest of mountain rode the horse trainers and old women who still have their own teeth.

"Am I to be a widow? If so, then embroider me a little pillow for my widow's tears," Khatun told the Bek's wife, Essin, who had gone to take some radishes from the servants to be washed.

"Who says you're going to be a widow?" Essin said hoarsely. "I'm just warning you there's going to be trouble again."

The prospect of something new circled in the air. Essin motioned with the back of her hand under her chin in the manner of the Baghdadi women. "The Caucasus must be free for the horseman of the mountain."

"Where do we Khazari fit in?" Mother told her.

"See Mount Elbrus in back of me?" Mother pointed to Essin. "That's the resting place of Noah's ark before it finally parked at Mount Ararat over the hill in the territory of the Armenians."

"There are rumors," Essin sighed. "Mountain Jews…most of them Persian, some from **Kwarizm** or Armenia. The other groups are diverse, some are Khazari. They're coming here. And the many tribes of the North Caucasus are trying to find out how to be included in their way of life."

The Pechenegs north of Kiev had gathered again to fight the Kievan Rus who now had teamed up with the Vikings. They sailed long ships down the Volga. Mother Russia, our open grassland steppes to the rest of the world, had now become an enemy country instead of the old bridge that connects all peoples to the eagle's nest dwellers of the Caucasus. And now our people were here, moving in on them, intruding, when we already had Khazaria.

Khatun warned Essin. "Do you think we'd be better off in Khazaria where the Kievan princes are invading our lands every time the sun goes down?"

"Didn't you hear what happened in wild-horse pastures?"

"No I didn't. Are we welcome here or not?" Khatun asked in a soft voice.

The village was safer than the cities in time of war. What could happen in the secure house of a man's childhood? Multitudes of black, long-haired goats browsed among the rocks. White, broad-tailed sheep nibbled the plants of the hillsides. Small oxen grazed in the valleys and the larger buffaloes wallowed in the marshes.

The wealthy herdsmen counted their animals by the thousand. The Kagan welcomed the visit of the mountain people's leader, Omar by raising his right hand to his head and lifting his cap.

He kissed the hand of the stranger of distinction and placed it on his forehead. Their wives met each other by a gentle embrace with their right arms, and then a clasping of their right hands.

Many of the tribes remained pagan, true to their ghosts of white horses in a pasture of cloud-whipped birch trees. Omar, the new leader of the village who rode the Silk Road all the way from Khwarizm, also had been to Persia, and now belonged to the people of the book.

"How did I come to this place?" The Kagan spoke these words in front of mother and me with a kind of ceremonious amazement. Omar sat before us and brought his wives to our women's quarters. "So you'll eat with our rabbi?" Khatun asked the leader.

"Of course," he said, nodding. "I'd give two of my best horses for Khazar game hens roasted with raisins and honey."

"And you will eat with us on Rosh Hashanah." The Kagan added as he majestically walked through the halls to meet the visiting leader. Father had a twinkle in his dark eyes and spices rubbed into his black beard and drooping moustache. The beard flowed to his waist. The Kagan wore Taklamakan's gift, a Khorat silk blue-green tunic.

On his arm crouched a flame-pointed Persian cat.

"Sing, 'Ride to Me, My Pecheneg Bride,' once more, Omar," a loud woman's voice echoed through the dark halls. It was the goddess of Silk, Queen of the Steppes, Taklamakan. She's the queen who smuggled silk worm eggs in her long hair and brought them here for us to trade in silk along with her people who have been allies with us for the last six hundred years.

A princess of Khotan gave the Steppe Queen, Taklamakan all her secrets of making silk. The Queen's brother also took more silk worm eggs hidden in hollow bamboo staves. His mind was on trading silk. The Queen had sent her twin brother in marriage to the princess of Khotan.

Not six weeks had passed, when before his wedding the prince ran away.

The eggs hatched into worms. The worms spun cocoons. By the time the caravan reached the Sea of Meotis, (where the Volga flows into the Caspian, the Sea of the Khazari) the women of the mountains and the steppe tribes were in the silk business with everyone except Byzantium. They had their own silk trade.

So the Queen of the Steppes, smiling, saw the Chieftain and took a sudden interest in her felt boots and indigo silk robes. Of all the Steppe's's women, Taklamakan would never wear animal skins, not even in the winter's cold of the steppe.

"Don't tell me you're shy," Khatun addressed, Taklamakan, the Queen of the Steppes. "Imam," the Kagan interrupted. "The Queen is looking for a husband. She came first to the Khazari. Now, she will look over your people."

"What's lacking in your own strong men that you come to us?" Omar dared to ask.

"Lacking?" Taklamakan shrieked. "Nothing's lacking. I'll tell you why I'm walking among your people. I need someone to take a journey for me—a long journey. If he returns, he may have the honor of marrying the Queen of the Steppes."

Mount Elbrus and Kazbek of his childhood terrified my father even in the days when he lived in far-off Derbend. Atil he knew from adulthood. Atil had a flat, dry steppe to it. Atil and Sarkel had no mountains, only the rivers, and Atil faced the Caspian, the Khazar Sea, where the Volga River flowed into it like the fingers of a hand.

For a long time some vague impatience had been gathering here, far from Atil. Father told me each day that he wished he could repair a mistake while there was still time. His Mountaineer allies, along with the tribes of the north and south mountains where the Volga meets the Sea of Meotis, the Pechenegs, and the peoples on the move along the Silk Road caravans had long battled the conquering Kievan princes on their West and the pastoral nomads on the East.

To the south lay the burning embers of defeated Rome and their eastern empire where the great libraries rose in Byzantium. And in the south Caucasus, were the Jews of Armenia and Persia who still sent emissaries to the great libraries of Baghdad for rabbis who knew the ancient Babylonian rite, the pizmoun and the nigun, the song prayers, and scholars to creep ever northward into the Crimea.

"To bag five princes on one arrow," the Bek, Bulan shouted to his Mountaineer ally. The Queen of the Steppes wandered here, among the men, still looking for a husband to replace the one she lost in battle a year ago and left her without sons at her still youthful age of eighteen summers.

"Who will marry the Queen of the Steppes?" the Bek laughed, looking at my father and the men gathered before the family for the great feast of sweets at Rosh Hashanah.

"Who will sit under this thatch-roofed sukkot, this grass-roofed lean-to, with me and find that Queen a husband?" The Kagan answered the Bek.

"Step toward me, anyone? You, the tarkhan, do you want a wife?"

"You know she won't have any interest in our faith," the tarkhan, our commander of the armies, replied.

My father continued, "She's still camping on my doorstep and glowering at my nine sons."

"What's wrong with a Mountaineer husband for her?" The tarkhan gestured with his hands like an eagle. "Aren't there enough males among the Steppes? Why is she not looking to her own peoples first?"

"She says she wants a man taller than herself," my father replied. "Is it our fault if she towers above her own men?"

"A tall man she wants?" The tarkhan laughed.

"Then let her look in places where the men are tall.

Why does she make things so complex?"

"The only tall men here are the Chechens to our north or all the way back in Kiev among the princes who invade our lands," the Kagan scowled.

"What the Queen of the Steppes should meet is a Rus Viking. See what you can bring from those long ships of the Vikings plying the Volga, the next time you're back in Atil," the Bek, Bulan answered.

"No," shouted the Kagan. "You can't bring our enemies here to marry the Queen of the Steppes. Her lands are just across the river from our lands. You don't want allies of the Kievan princes so close to our summer home up in the mountains. And you don't want them near Atil. The Caspian will always be the Sea of the Khazar."

"The Azeri men are tall," the Bek said as he crouched over the hot coals, roasting his mutton on a skewer.

"But they have broad skulls around the forehead," the Kagan said. "The Queen will have to measure the man's forehead so she won't die in childbirth like a previous Khazar princess named Chichek might have done after she married that Byzantine Emperor more than a hundred winters ago and then disappeared after her baby was born. A year after her disappearance, the Emperor had a new wife. She's not going to marry a man who doesn't have a narrow forehead. And for that, she must look to the Mediterranean peoples or to Persia."

"Or the star of the Indus," the tarkhan added.

"And the men we have here," I announced to my father and his leaders, "far outnumber the women, in spite of so many wars." I couldn't think of one man who wasn't afraid to marry the Queen of the Steppes, regardless of her beauty and youth. Since her husband had disappeared in battle, no one knew whether he would return.

"Go and ask of every tribe to send her a worthy son to choose," the Kagan commanded. "Maybe then, she will leave my handsome sons alone. They are all too young to marry anyone."

Women in steppe culture often hold positions of great power. Look at Parsbit, the Kagan's mother, deposing the previous tarkhan and appointing a new one. To the east, the steppe women fight alongside their men. The news I heard last summer along the Silk Road is that in the Mongol empire, women are regents.

When my father's brother escorted one of the Mongol Khan's wives to visit her father, the Byzantine Emperor sent word to her to put on a veil and conceal herself only when entering Byzantine territory. She never had to cover her head or face while in her husband's court or among the Turkic tribes who live just west of the Mongols.

I can't understand why Rome used to send people to be bitten by lions or have gladiators fighting one another and then dare to call our steppe people the barbaricum.

This name is given to anyone who wants land and food and whose women serve as regents. Our women appoint generals like our tarkhan to command the armies.

There are two free peoples here, those of the steppe, and those of the Kafkas. All the rest keep their women bound and gagged. Our women, literally, wear the pants. We have to, or else we couldn't ride our horses upside down to escape their arrows.

In the western Caucasus the various tribes such as the Kabardian, Shopsug, Cherkessk, Ubighye and the Adigye, who are the Caucasus Mountaineers, live under a form of feudal and aristocratic social organization. But in the eastern mountains, among the Lesghi, the Chechens, and the people of Derbend that some call Dagestan, there is no distinction of classes. We Khazari, come from a homeland in Derbend.

"Let the Queen walk among the Tatar tribes governed by their own khans," My mother put her opinion in the group.

A Tatar from our circle of friends shouted. "No! Our Tatar government is despotic. We have such a spirit of personal independence and moral self-sufficiency. We are all associations of free brothers. I don't want others ruling over us. I don't care how beautiful she is. Our Tatar brides are equally beautiful."

In time of peace all of us are brothers and sisters, free and equal before the law, with only such diversity of social condition as might result from a difference in natural gifts and the favors of fortune.

"Then we shall have a contest for a man to step forward worthy of being the husband of the Queen of the Steppes," the Kagan motioned to the Bek.

"Let her choose. If she makes an error, she won't blame us later."

"Let's go ask of the Kavkaz Mountaineers. They have contests," said the Bek. "Whoever had been endowed with most commanding powers, whoever was foremost in valor and the exercise of all manly virtues, was in fact a chieftain without an election.

He was king without a title. There is no difference among our brother tribes between natural and divine right."

The Bek chose Atokay, a free man of the Caucasus, to join at his own will with the other freemen to sit in a council ring on the green beneath the peach trees.

"We'll work with the Mountain Men in these meetings," my father said. "No officer will claim precedence as a right. These Caucasus mountaineers all grant it by consent to the elders and the most distinguished speakers."

The wise man was one who was valiant in arms, the influential from worth of character. The assembly hung upon the sweet tongue of eloquence. Atokay, the orator rose to speak. The principal men in the tribe stepped forward and kissed his robe.

The son of his youth, dashed into the ring on horseback to harangue the assembly from the saddle.

The whole group of Khazari rode over to the places where the Mountain Men lived. Atokay dismounted. "The object of this meeting is to agree on an expedition against the enemy." Atokay started.

His favorite topic was on the oppression and cruelty of the Kievan Rus. As he spoke, Atokay mentioned the burnings and shedding of blood. The Mountaineer aoul had been laid low by the Kievan princes. The youth had been carried away, and the tribes driven back into the mountains.

Atokay's voice raged with indignation and wailed in the plaintive tones of sorrow. His eyes flashed beneath his shaggy, contracted brows. He clenched his fist to grasp his shaska.

The blood rushed and returned from his cheeks. His chest heaved with violently struggling emotions. "Can we count on the Khazari to help us?" Atokay asked. The Khazar Bek heard the low, half-stifled sobs, the irrepressible tears that trickled down the sunburned cheeks of the men's circle.

Teeth were clenched and brows knitted and sabres half-drawn while Atokay spoke. At pauses the crowd responded, "olan oldu" At the conclusion a shout of applause broke from the universal throat ringing the air until the hills gave it back the cry of "Khazari, Khazari," in boisterous accord. Then the circle broke into a dance that shattered the thin air and rustled the birches.

Governed by custom, the Kagan and the Bek searched for a book or a proverb that would give all answers and guidance to all the different tribes of the Kafkas, also called the Kavkas, the Vladikavkaz, or the Caucasus Mountains.

Whatever rules of conduct have been longest established and found to meet necessities are held most sacred.

"To execute laws, not to make them" shouted Atokay in defiance of the changing times creeping out of the hills at his throat. "Who is the enemy now? What shall we do when there is no longer anyone to fight?" Atokay argued.

"Blood even unto the fourth generation" The crowd went up in flames of emotion. "We demand the Caucasus Mountaineer's right of revenge," shouted Atokay.

"For what?" The Kagan's voice raised an octave. "We didn't do it that way in our Derbend homeland before we took to the steppe and landed in our orchards where the Volga meets the Caspian."

"For the oath taken on our amulets."

"Secure the fulfillment," Atokay demanded.

In Atokay's home, the Kagan and Bek found his amulet, the eagle, suspended from two Cherkessk kindjal sheaths. This Roman type of dagger stood on the wall next to a tapestry.

Atokay, the warrior who never trembled now began to agitate with dread. "Having deposited his kindjal, he will die and keep his word," the Bek whispered to the Kagan, my father as I watched from the shadowed lattice of an open door leading to the next room.

Atokay's kindjal is, as you say in your time, about two-feet long, fluted, double-edged, and straight.

It is similar to the Roman dagger. A kindjal, with its own personality, is the most prized possession of a Kafkas mountaineer. Stabbing lacks artistry and is considered a disgrace to both Khazari and Mountain Men. That's why the Romans used our short kindjal as they would a machine. They probably picked it up from us in the Caucasus. And we picked it up from the Greeks who got it from the folk of India who traded it West to Persia. Kindjals here are almost a cult.

Each mountain kindjal has a name and sprite of its own. You never go anywhere without it. Women have a smaller version. How else can you protect yourself from a crazed and rabid wolf or worse?

Atokay presented my father with his Shasqa, the sword of the Kafkas, and compared it to his kindjal. Everything went up for barter and trade. The Shasqa is slightly curved like an edge of the moon, not like the short, kindjal Roman dagger. Oh, why talk of swords and daggers? They are only symbols it has been said for the vertical expression of a horizontal desire to seek new land in order to expand.

When famine creates hunger, people of the steppes and the mountains seek land to till and orchards to grow. The Mountain men have their valleys of the apples, and we Khazari have our orchards. May the harvest be plentiful on each person's dinner platter under the garden thatched roof of the Sukkoth.

We like to eat in our gardens under the stars with only the grass-roofed lean-to sheltering our long dinner table and many guests on these warm early autumn nights. Here high in the mountains we found universal hospitality. Those we met in the mountains kept the door of every house open wide from one end of the year to the next all over this place as we do in Khazaria.

"You know our people," the Mountaineer Atokay assured my father with a wide smile. "We let any foreigner enter our country unharmed. You walk on my soil and thereby place yourself under the protection of any chieftain you may pick for your *konak* or guardian."

"We welcome the Khazari as liberators for our Caucasus. Liberate us from the Rus, from the Steppes, from all except ourselves. You have earned your right to be my brother," Atokay told the Kagan of the Khazari.

"The Khazari are hiding all around us," Atokay said darkly. "They are in the spider webs. Look to the corners of each room of your houses. The Khazari are there. They are in the smooth blade of my Cherkessk kindjal. They are in the breakfast eggs, and on the dry grass our goats eat."

"Atokay, my friend, what are you saying?" The Bek soothed him with his arm placed heavily on Atokay's shoulder. "We are here to protect you."

"We Mountain Men have always protected ourselves. Your fortresses face the sea or the rivers and will be destroyed one of these days. Our fortresses are hidden so high in the mountains, they cannot be reached unless we allow it."

"Oh, heavens! Protect our children from the Queen of the Steppes," another tribesman added."

"The Queen says the same about the rainbow Kaganate," said Taklamakan. She proudly rode into the center of the men's circle and signaled her horse to creep along the ground like a dog.

To every woman each soldier was just another woman's son. My father took seven men of the crowd in his house. The seven young soldiers were Mountain Men and were followed by three other Kafkas mountain men. The Mountain Men never failed to do honor to their chief, Atokay, by halfrising from their seat on his entrance into the room.

Atokay offered the Kagan meat with a bowl of mead and goat's milk. He refused it. "Not kasher. Not kosher. Sorry my friend." And he politely waved it away.

"Now I know where the Caliph of Baghdad found his aversion to wild boar. But lamb and goat? Eat, my Kagan. Or else you'll grow weak. I remember the days when you drank milk from your finest horses. What's the matter, now? Are you too good for my sheep?"

"Look, I care about what I eat, and besides, we have more important problems to solve."

They offered him wine, but he provided his own wine, carried by the Bek's men. The Mountain Men offered the Kagan's soldiers a gift of a portion from their own dish some meat and pastry.

My father provided his own food and always carried it with him. Other tribes entered the area. The name-roll sounded seven times.

Atokay's house was never closed by day, and a pile of logs was always blazing on the hearth in winter evenings. The guests of distinction were on arrival assisted by the Mountaineer host who said to them upon crossing his threshold,

"Henceforth consider my father as your father and my mother as your mother."

Atokay then with his own hands relieved the Khazari guests of their weapons and placed them on the wall. Only after repeated solicitations on the part of the guests, and when all others had taken their seats, did the Atokay sit down next to the Kagan of the Khazari. Atokay crouched down at a respectful distance on the floor. I helped everyone bring out the feast.

A maid brought the fresh spring water. The guests washed their hands three times like the Khazari. Then each man washed the other man's feet. It made no difference if the person next to him was Khazari or Mountaineer, Pagan or Rabbinate. An Imam from Persia had been at the feast and he washed Atokay's feet.

In a corner of the room by the side of the hearth was spread a silk couch with a red satin pile of cushions and coverlets brought from Persia. The tarkhan slept on guard by the doorway guarding my brother.

Atokay, chief of the Mountain Men and a traveler had observed the local custom of asking for a kid from the flock and an ox from the herd, shoes for his feet and a coat for his back. Even my father had heard of the three Mountaineer virtues: celebrity, bravery, and hospitality. The Khazari added a three more virtues now: righteousness, following the commandments, and charity.

In strode the Queen of the Steppes. "To me these people are a sharp sword, a sweet, tongue, and forty tables," she said with a sweep of her hands. The guests left and Atokay and father were alone with their wives.

Taklamakan, the Queen of the Steppes strode to where I sat and placed her hands around my neck modestly as if she were her sister. "I hear you want to be a warrior's bride," I told her.

Taklamakan's brilliant beauty was concealed as much as possible from the luxurious eye. In her white mantle the young queen's form was always graceful.

It was evening, and her presence next to me by the fire had never ceased to be a natural ornament and charm. Taklamakan is barely eighteen and already a widow for the past two years. I'm still too young to stop dressing my cat and my dog in clothing.

Oh, and the Kagan, my father has the self-possessed air of a Khazar king who spits on fear. The sentiments of war fire in his eyes, his distended chest, and a grace as he opened his mouth: "While the soul is in my mouth, this country shall never be given to the tribes of the

Steppes or the Rus. When I die, I can no longer help it."

The Queen of the Steppes laughed. "Your only vice is hatred of your enemy. Hatred leads only to the grave."

The Bek joined our circle, meekly poking at the fire with a sword. "Why are you really here with us now, Taklamakan? Why aren't you ever with your people?"

"Your contempt for foreigners, your jealousy of rival, your implacable love of revenge have in them only barbaric greatness, nothing of the petty meanness of the vices of the other tribes here and the times of peace anywhere. I pity you, Bulan."

"This holy war will lead our people out of the hands of the Rus and into hell," the Bek admonished the Queen of the Steppes.

"War, Bulan, is only truth known too late."

Taklamakan spat back at Bulan into the fire. The flame of war was originally kindled at the torch of religious belief. For one, Taklamakan's first husband was a disciple of the Kagan of all the Khazari.

He brought her into this inter-tribal circle of friends and allies. The Bek also had his Mountaineer friends. There was his wife Raziet, whose father was a Mountaineer, a great cadi in the aoul of Jarash in the khanate of Kurin. The lady was reputed to be the wisest alim or teacher of righteousness in the territory of the eastern Caucasus called Derbend.

Long ago, her family had married into the royal family of the Khazari. The chief of her tribe had the patriotic heart of a learned healer. On our journey we brought with us a new visiting rabbi and a great scholar all the way from Spire, in the lands of the Teutonic peoples and the Alsatians, the Germanic peoples. He spoke many languages and dialects and had lived in Alsace and Cologne, his family there since the days of the Roman armies.

The red-haired rabbi from Spire called himself Josef, son of Aaron ha-Cohen who once studied in Spain's aoul of Aragon. Josef is a young, still single man. He had traveled far in search of knowledge of the Khazari people. He came here in search of a bride when he would reach twenty-five winters, and that time he had reached today. Still no bride he could marry under the Chuppah. And the Queen of the Steppes looked for a suitable match in a husband....I couldn't introduce them. So my duty would be to find each a match made in—the Garden of Eden.

In the world we go in life after life, there is no gate that would dare separate the Pecheneg from the Queen of the Steppes from the Khazari or anyone else. We all come from and go to the same place. And nobody knows this more than I.

My father's best friend is this Mountaineer chief who had come to Jarash to preach a crusade in behalf of freedom. Immediately the report of this calling of all who supported him spread like wildfire through Derbend and the province of the Lesghi. Disciples came from afar to hear the new doctrine.

My father rallied the tribes of the Steppes and the Mountain Men and all the other tribes to catch the zeal of the Khazari, but each followed a different faith and purpose. We went into the wagons covered by leather and took a long journey across the Kafkas to a neighboring district of Kara-Kaitch.

I rode with my brother who sat next to the Queen of the Steppes. We carried the burning words from aoul to aoul until the fury of the people burst out in a general rising to repel the advance of the next future enemy. If it wasn't one enemy, it always was another. Someone was always trying to start a brotherhood and gather the seeds of rebellion instead of planting his own patch of land.

The Queen of the Steppes rode now side by side with the Kagan. The Khatun rode in a bier. Only one of my brothers was with us, the thirteen-year old one, and the Bek guarded me from the outside world while I rode in the inside in tortoise formation like the Roman army.

So the Queen of the Steppes found an Avar husband to be the new Khan of the steppe tribes on the eastern shore of the Caspian, the Sea of the Khazari.

We were all invited to the wedding of Taklamakan, Queen of the Steppes. Finally, she found a husband, named Jalek Baian, a descendant of the great Baian, from among the Avars. That name is different from the Pecheneg, Jelek. They are a Mongolian people who absorbed many of the Uygurs from Central Asia and formed a confederation of the Volga steppes.

The Avars are ruled by their Kagan, also called Khan, and many are named Baian and Jalek. The Queen's future husband comes from the eastern shore of the Caspian. So, this night we went to her fine wedding. At last, she would leave my brothers alone. They are two, beautiful, trim people who deserve each other. Yet something tells me they really don't like each other. And the wedding gifts? I bet they'll keep them even if their wedding feast doesn't work out.

What would befit an eighteen-year old Queen of the Steppes and her Avar betrothed? Fine saddles, of course, and a stable of white horses from the Kagan of the Khazari....

What she won't get is the present sent to me by an old friend of my father's from his Silk Road adventure days. From the forbidden cities in far away Tibet, a rare snow leopard, all mine, and overseeing six of my fine flame-pointed Persian kittens, the meow sisters.

Cats of Khazaria, and more cats have been brought to me.. I have my snow leopard now since she was two weeks old, but she has no mate, except the wolf cub I raised since it was five weeks old. Odd, but they really don't get along.

Nightfall is coming. So let the wedding drums of the Pecheneg, Karachay, Cherkess, Adigye, Dagestani, Tatar, and Avar roll their compelling tattoos of the mountains, for we have long ago left the mountains for the steppes and our orchards. We are no longer prisoners of the mountains, yet we savor safety within these stone walls.

As we stepped into the Queen's golden yurt, clashing cymbals and tinkling bells welled up like a baton in a one, two, one, two, three rhythm. The many girls with their finger zills played a rhythm of the leather-covered wagons of nomads, and the Khazari brought blossoms from their orchards.

But here, up in the high Kafkas, not many Khazari brought blossoms from the Volga.

Here, our Mountaineer tribesmen brought their fine-crafted boots and saddles. Everything was made for riding on long journeys. I hoped the Queen didn't take that as a hint to keep on moving along.

We only meant her great gifts of long-standing value that wouldn't wear out with time or travel. At the wedding, the music of lutes, lyres, and harps sounded. A nye and kanoun brought by our Persian guests wailed from one room. The *nye* had a nasal sound from its two pipes as it whistled in with its flat tone.

A trumpet blared. Then a chorus of men began to chant as they slowly marched down the aisle. Mountaineer maidens marched in white silk and tossed flower petals. Their pillbox hats shimmered in the light. Veils flowed down their backs attached to the hats and covered their hennaed auburn braided tresses.

The women and girls stood on each side of the aisle in Taklamakan's onion-shaped yurt. The bride and groom sat on gold tasseled cushions. They rose and were led up several steps to the dais where two gold-winged thrones await them. The thrones were painted with the mythical Turkic hawks of Togrul. And in turquoise, gold, red, and white and covered with runes and tamgas of white horses, a gift from the Avars.

The Avars painted the Queen's throne with gold leaf. She ordered her blue gems imbedded on portions of the throne in areas that do not actually touch or poke at the bodies of those seated there.

Her groom's Avars mounted the gems on the throne on the sides and back or on the sides of the arm rests or throne legs. We helped to drape ancient royal hawk emblem of Togrul above the throne.

Also her servants draped over the thrones the cloth of the state, of many Turkic and other tribes that spanned the Kafkas and lands far across the steppes and the Silk Road. Her Avar betrothed placed above his throne a great golden-colored disk shaped like the sun with a white horse talisman similar to our Khazari tamga used before the conversion, in the middle.

Their Kagan and Khatun led the Queen of the Steppes and her Avar to the throne and seated them. They smiled and looked out at the guests. A designated official playing the part of their shaman removed the shimmering white and gold cloaks of the couple, hereafter called Khan and Khatun. Bet you can't say *Khatun* without clearing your throat or sneezing. My Khazar family flanked the royal couple. Following us were the Mountaineer maidens and the fan bearers in royal Tatar, Mountaineer, and Avar tunics.

Guests include attendants, soldiers, courtiers, and chamberlains. We had ordered food to feed Avar, Mountaineer, and Khazar soldiers, all males wearing their braids over one shoulder and females wearing their braids doubled in back. Each guest wore a special head dress to represent the country, rank, and title he represented at the great wedding of two tribes—Tatar and Avar.

Then the ritual began as the Avar royal cup bearer brought in their shaman's orange blossom-scented "holy" oil. The cup bearer dipped his fingers into the stone cup or jars and anointed each of the royal couple in the center of their foreheads.

I heard the thump of a goat-skinned Avar drum. A flute wailed its nuance in a minor key, keeping rhythm in a hypnotic dance, to the hand-drum beat. An attendant waves sheaves of wheat to the rhythm. Fan bearers slowly stirred the heavily incensed air. Astrologers arrived from the far away land of the Azeri.

Four Kaganates marched down the aisles—the Avars, the Tatars, the Khazari as wedding guests, and the Mountain Peoples. Steppe peoples and mountain peoples alike joined in the royal wedding. The Tatar and Avar regalia bearers marched slowly down the aisle.

They carried a hawk insignia on top of gold and white silk cushions with tassels. On one cushion, the Khan of the Avar peoples placed the great red and white hawk crown for the groom and on the other cushion is the great red and white crown for the bride.

An old talisman or tamga of a white horse was placed in the robes of the bride. Many years ago, such tamgas decorated the standards of the Khazari. Now, we have the menorah, and the star.

We are the wanderings stars of Atil who wander now only in our own orchards.

Custom is that the crowns and the emblems are extra heavy to emphasize responsibility and trust that the wearer must carry. The trust and responsibility were to the tribes.

Another regalia bearer marched down the aisle bearing symbolic hawks. These small hawks represent the mythical hawk, Togrul that the Pechenegs, Tatars, Avars, and several other tribes used to represent their flight to freedom.

The hawks are meant to be carried by the bride and groom or each of the royal couple. A regalia bearer behind the royal couple carried a cushion of gold with tassels on which the "golden hawk of Togrul" is borne. This is a small, striped hawk.

Two regalia bearers followed with a cushion bearing two scepters-- the white horse mounted on top of a royal Avar scepter for the queen, the khatun of the Steppes, and her Avar khan.

The last regalia bearer carried a cushion that held two "sacred horses" This is a replica of a "golden-carved horse of the steppes," one for each of the couple, shaped as a head dress.

The regalia bearer handed each golden horse replicas to the shaman of the Steppes who then placed the sacred hawk on the groom's head first and then on the bride's head. The two golden scepters with the white horse on top are then handed to each of the royal couple. The flutes and drums stopped. All became silent.

Each of the guests bowed down to the Avars, showing their allegiance as allies. It seemed as if the whole mighty Kafkas bowed to the confederation of tribes of the steppes. I wished the Pechenegs were here, but only one little boy from their peoples was here as now part of the Khazar family.

Everyone in the room bowed down, prostrating themselves on the floor with face touching the floor, knees bent. No one looked up as the great shaman of Togrul placed the hawk crowns on the

Khan and Khatun The custom of the Silk Road dictates that anyone looking up is cursed. They each waved their horse talisman scepters, and the drums rolled.

The shaman high priest began to chant his ritual pagan incantation. As his incantation started, the guests stood up. The music began first by cymbals clashing. Trumpets and flutes wailed nuances of the steppe and mountain people's delight. A chorus of singers sang wildly to the harps and other stringed instruments joined by the flutes, trumpets, and lyres, the handheld drums, tiny bells, and finger cymbals (zills), tambourines, and other tinkling sounds.

From Persia and Baghdad to the steppes came the nye flutes with their double pipes, and stringed harps, like the kanoun of Mosul. Drums of Abkhazia rolled so fast, they sounded like one trilled note. A chorus of singers chanted a mountain melody and then a song of the steppes.

The shaman began his exalted incantation. He announced the names of the royal couple and their titles. Then the couple took their oath: I, Taklamakan, Queen of the Steppes and confederation of Kaganates, Queen of the creator- and family-loving divine light within, the Ever living, solemnly pledge my sacred promise that as Khatun of Avaria and the steppe lands, and Liege of the Lands, I, of the House of Greatness, will uphold, maintain, and govern with all my creative powers, the customs of my realm, pledging my promise to my creators, my people, my responsibility, and my trustworthiness with the help of Togrul, and those of all the lands in my realm, until the day that I start a new life. All this I do vow as my pledge. The Avar Khan and the Alani, the Adyghe, the Karachaian, the Balkarian, all took the same pledge as khan. Only my father, Kagan of the Khazari, as a guest of the Judaic faith refused to pledge to the white horse tamgas and all the spirits of nature. We found friendship within the the wonderfully diverse and yet united tribes of the Caucasus with their many languages.

Someone placed a little white horse amulet in the Kagan's pocket anyway, and he didn't seem to mind. Again, he did this for a little extra good luck.

We all enjoyed the pageant and offered my wedding gift to the bride and groom and wished them good life. Our proper gift unfolded before their pleased smiles--fine fabric from the Silk Road and new fruit trees in their holders. Just for the road, the food wasn't koshered, but we enjoyed the grains and fruits that we saw had been boiled in fresh spring water.

Their shaman addressed the royal couple as a house of greatness and asked them to take their Oath of Fealty. He asked each to repeat, "I give you from the Three Estates: Our priesthood, nobility, and people in the name of the horizon of the sacred hawk of Togrul, most select of places."

Soon the royal ambassadors from other lands and nobles approached the wedding thrones. This is not exactly my brother's conversion back in Atil. Yet there was a similarity in the dance of the Avars. It was just like our own wedding dance, and looked like this—only with the rippled drum trills like the mountain peoples play:

Each of the nobles gave the prostration. Then they bent down on one knee with the other leg stretched out sideways with the right arm in a clenched fist pointing to the left chest as a salute and head bowed.

A line dance began that looked like our own wedding dances. Here, look at that line of males dressed as soldiers walking bended knee with the right arm, fist clenched, to the chest, and then saluting outward and back as they move, crouched down, in a straight line down the aisle.

Their left leg is bent at the knee in a deep knee bend, while the right leg juts out forward as they inch down the aisle toward the thrones, moving slowly to the musical rhythms of flute, *nye* of the Levant, harp, and the tattoo of the rolling hand drums from the mountains.

The line dance halted at the boots of the royal couple now wed and crowned at the same time, as the tribes of the north Caucasus do at royal weddings that are also coronation pageants where they take their royal oaths again when married anew.

The nobles chanted. Then the khan and khatun took their oath: They repeated, "I take the oath and vows to my lord (and lady) as a sacred compact between you, the rulers invested with the crowns of Avaria and the lands of the Tatars, who are now many peoples and our allies, and we, the ruled according to the ancient laws of our kingdom."

Their shaman chanted their titles and sang the oath. "I now invest you with the divine light of the great who came before you, living image of Togrul, children of the hawk and the horse, the chosen of the steppes, the heavenly star of the East.

"Nightingale of all the tribes, the soul and the word, Creator-loving, family-loving goddess and god, divine light, young khan and khatun, lifegiving creator of the new and bridge-bearer of the ancient, tradition of traditions, wisdom of the serpent of knowledge and choice: May you reign in serenity, reach for the stars, and may you live forever. All-encompassing net, joiner of souls, fisher of time, all-knowing catcher of dreams, remover of space, and connector of generations: May you live forever more.

All people present repeated this incantation after the shaman backed away in silence. The whole assemblage with one voice repeated the incantation of the priest once, and then, all together. The chorus of voices welled up wishing the couple "May you return forever, the soul's beloved."

The Shaman spoke, "May you live forever. Hail Khan of the Avars and Tatars, and Khatun. May your divine light live forever. Health, prosperity, and life. May she live. May he live—everlasting, forever."

The royal couple now rose. The attendants removed all the mantles and royal robes. Only the floor-length tunics and head dresses remained on them. Their greeted their guests wearing only a floor-length pale blue garment with a thin white robe over it. The heavy crowns now went away with the regalia bearers. The royal couple slowly walked down the aisle as the music welled up. Look now. Look over there to your right. The children are tossing flower petals in their path.

All subjects kneeled and prostrated themselves. The royal couple followed by individuals and crown-bearers walked by. Then they assumed a bowed-head position, clenched right fist to chest with one leg thrust outward to the right side. They saluted and remain bowed as the royals passed by moving down the aisle. We emphasized being polite to honor all the traditions of these mountains and rivers. You never know when you need some help.

The subjects remained kneeling. The regalia bearers handed a bouquet of flowers to each of the royal couple. Their shaman now rose from his kneeling position half way down the aisle. He is meeting the royal couple. The Queen of the Steppes and her new Khan took the flowers and placed them on an altar.

Then the royal couple each bowed in front of the altar and placed incense into the flame. We saw the shaman poke at the flame and throw more incense on it. The regalia bearers helped everyone decorate the room at the end of the aisle as a miniature Avar temple.

Isn't it interesting that when Pagans become another faith, so much of the customs remain the same, like striking up a flame or putting incense on a burner or washing with the water of orange blossoms before entering a house of prayer? We have a motto that the more things change, the more they stay the same, and that motto is known all over the world.

The royal couple turned and walked down the aisle and onto their balcony. They faced their people outside cheering the royal wedding. There, they made their appearance to the masses of people in the street below. As they waved, the crowd sank to its knees and bowed deeply. The crowd cheered. "Hail, hail. May the Khatun live forever! May the Khan live forever!"

The shaman and a female relative of the royal couple entered the balcony to join the royal couple standing there facing the public. The shaman and female relative were followed by a regalia bearer with a gold cushion. Taklamakan's sister removed a gold wreath from the pillow and crowned the shaman with the long black braids with her gold wreath.

The Khatun of the Steppes's sister, Minay, took a sack of precious gems and poured them onto a table on the balcony to show the shaman. She dropped the baubles into a gold silk bag. Minay handed the gems to the shaman of the Tatars and Avars as a gift.

A crowd of many tribes cheered wildly. They approved. Shamans nodded and bowed all the way to the floor. The royal Khan and Khatun retreated from the balcony. They stepped up to sit on a bier. Soon eight bearers carried them down the aisle for the rest of the way until they disappeared from sight.

Taklmakan and her new husband entered a golden litter and sat on two gold-colored chairs. Bearers carried the couple in a procession followed by marching Avar, Tatar, Mountaineer, and Khazar soldiers in front and in back. The soldiers were followed by marching shamans of the various tribes who carried regalia and emblems.

In the order of procession, the first litter carried the relatives of the royal couple, the second litter, the royal couple, and the third the nobles. Guards followed in the rear of the three litters. This was a wedding of the steppes, the Caspian, and the Kafkas to be remembered, with many tribes and peoples. It seemed as though the whole salad bowl of peoples from every corner of the Silk Road and the Caspian came to the wedding—from Abkhazia to Derbend, and from the Volga to the Dnieper.

Above, the sun was huge and golden as it glinted off wedding guest's golden robes. The wedding party glowed like fire as if they were children of the sun.

The winding procession moved along wide streets followed by many musicians who clashed cymbals, bells, and finger zills (finger cymbals.)

Drums never ceased their fast trills and compelling tattoos. The flute players followed the drummers, and then the lute and harp players, a chorus of singers, and the *nye* players (two-pipes on the flute). Khatun and Khan sat on cushions on the golden chairs in the litter. They finally leaped from the litter and walked up the steps to the dais.

Again, the royal couple sat on the thrones chanting sacred songs along with ever-growing chorus of voices welling up as the sun glowed orange-gold.

One chorus is composed of men and the other f young females. The royal fan bears moved on each side of the royal couple. At last I heard the chorus of voices all the people who stood outside to cheer the wedding.

Soon, the music faded, until I heard only the hand-drums. Now, my father, the Kagan, moved forward and lighted a centerpiece oil lamp of lightness and joy in the middle to light up the dark and bring the joy of the lightness of being, the joy of blending dance with the expressiveness of worship with fervor into the dance that brings people together at a wedding or other joyful event.

Children danced into the center ring inside the innermost circle. They clapped their hands, twisted, and turned, down on one knee, arms on one another's shoulders, moving along in a line, like a wedding ring or circle of life. As the dance began, the Khazari who happened to be in the area and wanted to join in the dance wore their own fringed cloaks bearing "tzitzzes" (fringes at the bottom).

The tzitzzes shivered in the wind as the dancers bent on one knee, twisted around to the left and right, snapped their fingers, and leaped high into the air, lifting their own dancers on their shoulders and dancing with them in circles. They danced and danced and moved farther and farther away until they came to their own place in the woods where they danced until dawn.

And when the sun came up again, the Khatun of the Steppes and Avars had not gone anywhere to celebrate their wedding. Soon they'd return back to their fourth century golden age and out of our ninth century where they had merged into the settled peoples who came from east of the steppes. What they'd leave would be the song of the steppes, fragrant blossoms of the Silk Road and silver bracelets.

They were with us. We weren't alone, again. Suddenly I sensed the warmth of my own Khazar close-knit family. And that it was my duty as a princess of righteousness to welcome the Queen of the Steppes and her family into mine. What a blessing to be as closeknit a family as we are. I knew I must now honor our differences as the variety that has been created in the world by our almighty. And by the arrival of the Khazari I, too, must help the oppressed everywhere gain their honor and freedom through charity.

The Queen of the Steppes wouldn't let me kasher or kosher her kitchen again, but she let me paint her portrait in crushed rock, ochre, and egg yolk.

"Raziet-Serakh, my little Turkic flower of the Caspian," she said in a calm voice.

"I'm also a Jewish princess now." I added. "I need to take a Hebrew name. I'm supposed to forget I used to be Raziet-Serakh of the Caspian. But why should I forget my beloved Alania?"

"Oh yes. I see. You don't have to forget. Just include. We are people of many lands. And what is wrong about being Raziet-Serakh, an ally to everyone? Isn't memory about love? We are all your family."

"We will always be your allies and friends, steppe sister. Your people have merged into almost all lands now."

Taklamakan peered at me as we shared the table for our evening meal with this beautiful eighteen-year old newly wed. "Do you want to know how the ancient Tribes restored purity to Rome by destroying the corruption in it?"

I wanted to hear the tribal side of their story. "I'm all ears, steppe sister."

"When the Khazari first became allies of the Tribes, the Romans shrank the world of the Tribes like the most delicately tinted of bubbles, shrinking in ever narrowing circles from the upward gush of our own infancy." The Queen sat across the table on a wreckage of blankets.

"Is that why you chose the Avar to be your Khan and not my oldest brother?"

"Oh, come now, why would a Jewish Khazar warrior prince of Atil and Sarkel marry this boar-hunting Queen? Because our peoples have been allies for five hundred years?"

"Well, maybe if your father was a Cohen instead of a Khan…"

She laughed, amused by my humor. "You've got to be crazy to ask a steppe sister to tell your fortune. That's what you're painting, aren't you? My portrait is my fortune, is it not?"

Taklamakan's snarl curved into a snicker. "The seasons were dry. No rain for years. The crops withered. Then the animals perished. The climate turned very cold. No goats. No sheep. No horses to ride the steppes. We began to starve. The rains fell in the West. We had to feed our families. That was all there is to it. Not the mighty Roman reason that the famines of Central Asia destroyed their civilization. We have our own civilization of the steppe. We went west to find land where there was food and a place to live."

"And a lot of gold and booty to trade," I said laughing. "When nomads move, it's to trade. Look at the Vikings. Five hundred years ago the Tribes of the Steppes and the Caucasus did what the Vikings do today. You may be are allies, but you do look for booty to trade, and did so with Rome. Did you take all the scrolls from the libraries there? No. You took the gold."

"We took the scrolls."

"The Byzantines said you burned the libraries and melted the gold."

"Gold buys scrolls."

"Who's teaching you to read the scrolls?"

"I read in seven languages."

"You're the Queen."

"That's why we hire Khazari to tutor our children. Romans were making slaves of the

Tribes and their allies. We're as good as they are. We did go to their nation to learn."

"To burn."

"No, we taught them how to ride in battle our way. They hired scribes to write it all down in scrolls that went out along the Silk Road."

"Maybe it's time to learn more than how to fight."

"Then you will conquer us if we let ourselves grow weak and read until our eyes are dim. What would all that book learning do for us when our eyes went bad and we forgot how to ride to escape the arrows of our enemies?"

"You could be healers like the Kagan and his oldest son."

"Then the Caliph would make us his slaves so we could heal the royal family in his lands; or if not him, than the Emperor of the Byzantines, or the Sultan in Egypt. What about the Rus and the Pechenegs? What about your people?"

"Do you want me to paint your hair with this ochre-- orange or black?"

"Why are you painting my portrait?" Taklamakan asked me.

"I want to observe you. I observe life. I don't really live it, not in the way you do."

"When you paint my face, you paint my destiny and my fortune."

"No, I don't. I paint your memory. I can look on it when I'm old."

At that moment, her new husband, the Avar, Jalek Baian, the third walked through the door.

"Where were you last night? You weren't in your room this morning."

"Why do you always want to get your own way?" The Avar yelled back.

"What sacrifices a newlywed Queen has to make for her husband's education," she exclaimed with exasperation.

"You sure don't sound like a newlywed." I moved back from the table and sat in the corner to finish her portrait.

"Why did you marry your Avar prince?"

"My wife marries men for their shock value," he said to me.

"Jalek Baian, you're my dad reincarnated,"

Taklamakan shot back. "You're not my Khan. Some demon's got into you. Look how angry your eyes are. No, you're not the wolf cub I just married. It's time to say goodbye. Your eyes tell me my own future."

"Maybe you two are just incompatible souls," I interjected as I watched Jelek Baian sit down to ravage a piece of meat on a skewer.

Taklamakan shuddered at the noise he made eating the roasted leg of lamb cut in chunks and put on small wooden sticks between small onions.

"If the Khazari hear you complaining about me, I'm going to take many more wives," Jelek said. "I have a right to marry as many wives as I please. I'm the Khan of my own peoples now."

"Everybody wants to be the Khan," I whispered to my horse.

"And I'm still the Queen."

Taklamakan rose to look over the portrait that I now had finished. I painted her riding her horse with the wind through her long hair. I drew her as wild looking as her horse with the same expression in the eyes. It was a longing for the freedom of the steppe.

She spoke to her husband as she waved my painting above her head to view it from all sides.

"You are my father reincarnated. When I was born, the midwife announced to him that he now had a new daughter. He told the midwife to look twice.

'Are you sure it's not a boy?' he asked."

"Shaddup, shaddup, you werewolf of the steppes, the Khazari will hear you." Jalek groaned.

"You're going to make me kill you."

Taklamakan ignored him and looked me straight in the eye for sympathy. The more sympathy she could get from me, the more she manipulated me with anger.

The Queen of the Steppes meant trouble. I tried to help her. I tried to force pity so I'd give her a ride someplace on my steed. She said she wanted her independence again.

"I must leave here," she said quietly. "I have chosen the wrong husband to be the Khan of my peoples. I will ride alone until I find the right man to be the father of my future children."

"I won't give you children. You're not going to rule me," Jalek said as he turned away.

"Why do you speak to me only in commands?" Taklamakan sobbed. "I'm the Queen. Why isn't anyone listening to me?"

"Not since you made me the Khan of your peoples and mine."

"Isn't it funny how our marriages always turn out to be like our parent's no matter how much we try to be different?" Taklamakan said.

No matter how bad the marriage went, those two types would be hardest to separate. In their mood swings, they could kill each other.

"Never marry a timid man. The shy one will explode in anger at his wives," she told me.

"What would I know about marriage at fifteen?"

"The shy ones observe everything and turn it inwards, putting themselves down, calling the partner a loser, and finally, bursting with violence when they start to feel sorry for themselves."

It was obvious our whole family said that Taklamakan controlled Jalek with an iron hand inside of a velvet glove. When he was free of her a few hours a day, he went way over the limit.

"I like you, Raziet-Serakh," Jalek said to me meekly.

"That's too bad," I answered defiantly. "I don't like you. I like friends my own age, friends that I can run and play with and trust with my life that they won't curtail my own freedom to think for myself and question all who seek power."

"That's right. We are both thinking women," Taklamakan added. "Women destined to be the Khatun of each of our lands."

He exploded. "I hate this room where you play. I hate the cold fireplace, and your vicious wolf cubs. I hate every pelt in this room."

"Jalek, don't do this," I said. "You're coming to live with me to see how it works out," Taklamakan said. "We've only been married one day."

"I hate everything in this room, from the kettle that holds the kindling you never use to the dumb statue of a wolf that has a history I've heard too many times." Jalek ran to the mantelpiece and tossed everything to the carpet. He took a vase with an oil lamp in it and threw it at the Queen. Taklamakan ducked, but the vase flew through the window.

"He's being ugly," she shrieked to me. "And he smells like rotten apples."

Jalek ranted on. "At your wedding it was the two deaf ladies from Atil that I had to entertain.

"I'm so lonely, I could die." Suddenly he was ashamed of what he'd blurted out.

"My wedding? The wedding was for us."

Jalek the third, Khan of the Avars, looked at me shocked that I'd see inside him. A servant girl poured some nettle tea into several chalices and handed me and him a cup. "Please, let's all be friends," I said cautiously.

The herbal mixture on the table stood untouched. "I hate the two, long, watery drinks that have to last through the night," he teased, twisting his mouth. "I hate the phony smiles in this room. You're all laughing at me. I'm sick of the fake formality you go through to impress me, my ladies."

"You've done pretty well tonight helping him to talk, to open up like a woman," Taklamakan complained.

"All I see are phony, stapled smiles, like costume dolls," Jalek continued. "Two red dots on each cheek."

The Queen of the Steppes couldn't show anger. "Maybe if you had to go out and till the land for a living instead of living for the moment."

"What about you?"

"You worry me so," Taklamakan cried. "It's a barrier to the pain you cause me. You disappeared on our wedding night. Where did you go? And today, you want me to leave. Why don't you leave? I want a new husband, maybe a match from one of the sons of the Kagan of the Bikhar Khazari."

"Maybe you want your freedom." I interrupted.

"What do you know, steppe sister? You're only fifteen."

Jalek the third took up his goblet. "Shove your time-traveling trip. I want something of my own."

That was the first faint surge of triumph he'd felt all evening. "Nothing makes a tribal queen angrier than to have her youthful husband argue like an old hen," Taklamakan said.

"Tonight I'm ready for a fight," said the Avar Khan.

"Save your energy for the Pechenegs," his wife said darkly.

"You control every facet of his life. He is a king to his people. Why don't you let him show what he can do for his own people?" I asked her.

"The wrong husband can ruin your whole wedding day," she said. "Why won't he allow me a life?"

"Allow?" I hesitated.

My mother heard it all from behind the drapery and entered the room, uninvited. Her royal presence acted to calm down the couple.

"Does he expect you to say 'My dear little baby, don't grow up?'" Khatun announced as she rustled her cloaks and lighted the oil lamps.

"Taklamakan," Khatun said. "Jalek is asking what children always ask."

"What's that?"

Jalek walked toward my mother. He put his powerful tanned arms around her. "If I fall in battle with the Pechenegs, then will you love me, mommy?"

Jalek broke down in tears. "Tell her, Khatun. Tell her."

Mother blew a long sigh through the serrations of her lower teeth. I've taken in a Pecheneg orphan, an Avar, and now you. Sit down. My table is ample enough to feed one more mouth. Besides, charity multiplies.

"We just found out today. Jalek is going into a battle and is vastly outnumbered." She told the whole family at the dinner table.

Jalek crumpled, sobbing at mother's feet. "I'll never be a man."

Taklamakan poured the goblet of herbs and water over the back of his neck. "You wimp, get up. Thousands of people win battles with the Pechenegs. You have to be a man if you want to ride with the Queen of the Steppes."

"I'm going to end up defeated."

"Defeat is an opportunity for change. You don't have to go into battle, though, and you don't have to take the coward's way out. Join our secret time-traveling family."

"It must take a lot of doing to win all that strength over into your own corner and then go on eating at the same table, living normally day to day," Jalek told me.

He arose and looked at Taklamakan and I. "You two steppe sisters are too good at everything, like my step mom—training a wild horse or riding upside down or cooking dinner for twelve hundred without servants."

"Tell me about your real mom, Jalek. When I was your age, talking wasn't an option," Khatun said.

Like a thorough bred horse, I could see immediately that Jalek couldn't resist the challenge. Before he could open up to me in front of us, Taklamakan interrupted and cut him off in the middle again just as her own father did to her. She told me all about her life raised by a widowed Khan and trained to ride and use a curved sword from the age of five.

"I seek the wisdom of the Silk Road." Jalek sighed and fell silent. "Where's my father?"

"The Pechenegs killed him in battle." She cried.

"I saw a Pecheneg also named Jalek burned by the Kievan prince," said father.

"You saw Jelek, the Pecheneg. The Avar Khan's name is Jalek." I told my family.

"I didn't realize the Avars and Pechenegs had almost the same names for their sons."

"What are you thinking, mother?" I turned to the Khatun. "Don't let the sound of a name fool you. Similar sounds may have different meanings among a variety of peoples. I knew a Kievan prince's son also with the same name. And then there was a Bulgar named Jelek. What about the merchant from Khwarizm named Jalek?"

"I say the Khan's a spy. He's no Avar. Look at his face sideways. He's a Pecheneg."

"Do they really look that different? They have so many different people who joined them along the Silk Road. They could look like anybody here. He could be a Uyghur or an Oghuz," mother insisted.

"Taklamakhan," I sighed. "Do you really want to stay married?"

"My father always called me a thinking woman," said mother. "So now think for yourself clearly, Taklamakhan. Do you want to stay with your husband? Do you want him to go to war? Or do you all want to lay aside your feelings and join our family time-traveling through the centuries and find out what real wars have turned into so that you may go home and avoid them?"

Taklamakan thought how I could tell her that she had to really love herself and respect herself to deal with all the worry. How could I treat this war on a family level when a bigger war was going on outside the door, a war of hatred between the haves and the have-nots, the culturally different, and even the whole world?

As much as war stank, it was responsible for the evolution of knowledge. Not that knowledge is wisdom, but that righteousness is wise. There's a fine line between knowing how to heal or knowing how to pray or knowing how to build a weapon or wagon with more wheels that doesn't break or a horse that can gallop through a desert like a camel.

That bothered Taklamakan a lot. The last time we two steppe sisters feasted together, an old lady got ahead of her in line as we waited in the hot sun for a goat skin bag of water to drink.

Taklamakan grabbed the lady who cut in front of her and screeched, "Get out of my way before I push in your face." All that inner rage exploded.

At home, the Queen of the Steppes was incapable of showing anger. Instead, she'd make you feel guilty by prying your sympathy at how sick she was with loneliness at eighteen. With a total stranger whom she was sure of never seeing again, she pinched and shoved and stepped hard on toes.

All the anger she banked for years, but told me about since we were children traveling backwards in time together was suddenly spent on a stranger.

"Was I the goddess of the steppes?" She laughed afterwards in her shaky voice. There weren't many goddesses in the steppes, just our mythical hawks, horses, amulets and the spirits in the trees. Taklamakan is smart. She changed the subject.

"We're placing power in sick hands. Half the Khans of the Steppes have slapped their concubines around or worse. Our people are creating cages too small for a couple to hide in. Everybody knows two wolves in a cage bite each other. So do two people in a small campground yurt."

The Queen of the Steppes is a little doll face with blood-red lips. "Do I have to drive a stake through his territorial line? Must I mark the path across his river to stop him from mothering me?"

She always asked me this kind of a question. Then she answered it herself with a 'but.'

"Would you want to have your daughter marry a great Khan exactly like you?" she added. "Just walk out, Jalek and don't turn back. I prefer to stay with this large extended family of Khazari until I decide what I want to do. That's the only way I'll remain Queen of my people."

Jalek couldn't stop laughing. Taklamakan was serious. Mother told her. I've told her. She wouldn't listen.

He couldn't believe it. "Taklamakan to live with a Khazar family?" Jalek choked on his water laughing so loud, so strained, and so fake.

Mother pleaded with the Queen of the Steppes to spend the night. "Come, daven with us. Pray with us," said mother.

'I'm afraid of Jalek," she sobbed. "He's cruel--like his dad, and just as miserly."

"So that's it," I said loudly. "It's all about wealth."

The makeup Taklamakan slapped on her teenage face looked like a clown. Her shiny black hair flopped under the flickering oil lamps.

Taklamakan is like a second daughter to my mother, the Khatun. She braided her hair when the Queen of the Steppes was a small child and we played together each time our peoples met in the steppes.

In a war, a prayer, or a marriage, something usually goes chaotic. Nothing can be planned to go a certain way. There's always the law of chance, the unforeseen, or the unstable. There's always something going awry on the fractal curve of life's number game. That's the way it is when you ride with the Queen of the Steppes. Keep your bags packed.

Jalek moved backwards, tearing the goblet from Taklamakan's grip, and flinging her wedding bracelets onto the ground with a vengeance.

"Do you honestly think these trinkets you gave me will give you back your manhood?"

Taklamakan laughed at him. "Or can only warfare achieve that?"

"Only you stand between me and my manhood."

He reached out to touch her, but she jumped away. Jalek took Taklamakan in his arms and grinded his mouth on hers, forcing her back. She pushed him away.

"It's wrong. So terribly wrong," she said sarcastically. Hopelessly, he released her.

"You're mighty bitter for having been married only one day, my Queen." He turned to leave the room, but she blocked his path and grabbed his shoulders.

"Why can't you look me in the eye? Why can't we talk anymore? You don't have to be my husband. We can talk. We can be friends," she demanded. "Now I realize I'm not looking for a husband after all. No, I don't want one. I want a friend. I want my mother. I need a shoulder to cry on."

He flung her into the wall, and her head knocked a tapestry to the carpet. He looked up in surprise to see the hole she had cut in his wall leading to hers. Jalek ran over and poked his finger through.

"You weak spy," he ranted. "You spied on me all this time. You were always watching me. You're a woman who can't take care of herself married to a man who can't take care of a wife—even if she is Queen of the Steppes."

"I'm too young, not too weak. Maybe it's time for us to go our separate ways," Taklamakan calmly told her husband in almost a whisper.

Our whole family now was in the room staring at the royal couple. Oh, how they must have dishonored themselves in front of our family.

She put her arms around him, but Jalek wrenched her wrist, twisting it so she dropped one of his trinket wedding bracelets.

Sobs convulsed the Khan's shuddering body. "I won't give you the satisfaction of getting revenge. I'll go quietly, my Queen."

She retreated at his words, but he followed her, suddenly aware of a pouch of coins he wore around his neck. He removed the sack and slowly put it on the table.

"I'm returning your parent's bride wealth. I'm glad they weren't here at this moment, and that our Khazar friends were, since they are neutral to our marriage."

"I am not an animal. I'm a man." He turned his back to her. "Do you see the tail of a dog? No. I'm not an animal."

Taklamakan crouched next to my skirts, cowering beside my table, her eyes wide with fright. Gibberish spilled from the twitching corners of her white-lined lips. The sounds angered him.

She wiped the white foam from the corners of her mouth. "I don't care if you leave," Taklamakan sobbed. "Jalek stole all my wealth and property. Now I have nothing. I'm a Queen without a country."

My father walked in. I heard his footsteps above and know he watches everything below from his secret window above. This is his rooftop eagle's nest. He has the view of a fish, at least when we have guests.

"Stay with us, Taklamakan," father asked.

"When you start to respect yourself again, you'll be part of our family. I have the solution to all your problems."

"Good bye." Jalek walked out.

"Let him go," I said.

Father took her hand and led her as he leads any of the large number of children in our royal Khazar family. "While you are still under twenty, ride the Torah of Time, the Steppes of Sanity, the Depths of Dreams, the Roads of Righteousness, and the Mountains of the Mighty with us.

"You'll see the Silk Road a thousand times in new ways. Time-travel and see the world in all its stages. The lesson you will have learned is that we all marry our mirrors--someone who reflects how we feel about ourselves at one moment of time. In another moment you might feel differently about yourself and choose another for an entirely different reason.

"Every wife is a mirror of her own husband's failures, and every husband a victim of his wife's success."

With that, Taklamakan began to think about what he said. "A wife can mirror her husband's successes too," she added. "And a husband can diminish with his wife's failures."

"It works both ways," father said briskly. "Give yourself time. All we can offer you in Khazaria is time. "Now let me show you our secret cave where you can travel and learn by seeing the world that the more things change, the more they stay the same. This irony has been etched in sandstone now for what is it—six thousand years?"

All of a sudden up came a whirlwind in the clouds, and we found Weasel Cave once more beneath some branches where we tried to camp for the night. We went through the labyrinths of stalagmites and stalactites. I left little pieces of silver lace fabric as markers so we could find our way back in day or night.

There was a dark cavern of sorts, and a fierce wind came up and pulled all of us through in a whirlwind. A funnel of purple gray dragged each one of us up along with our four horses and the queen's bier and her horses. From the ledge of a great calcite cliff, we flew into the blackness.

You see, we have been to this place and time traveled to the same scene of what happened to my Khazaria many times. And we take our guests here to show them what will be so that they will gain insight, foresight, and hindsight. Our secret is Weasel Cave.

The next instant a burst of sunlight blinded us for a few minutes, as we whirled through a large opening at one end and a small opening at the other. And suddenly we were on the outside of cave, but where were we? Nothing looked familiar.

And the noise: the incredible thunder and fire around us. We were strangers in a strange land, and time stood still. No, not quite. It moved drastically forward.

"We will be sold as slaves in this strange place," the Kagan shouted to the Khatun. The place was the same, but time shifted and moved its foundation. We were on the other side of time.

"Wait, let's find out."

Before we had time to recover our wits, there came a sound like the roar of lions and moved forward faster than anything we could have imagined. "Where are we?" I demanded, and no one had the answer—yet. All I knew is that we had awoken in another time, in the probable future, because our beloved Sarkel was destroyed, yet we were suddenly back in Khazaria in another time and in the middle of a war.

I later found out we had been swept more than one hundred summers into the future, when the Kievan prince had destroyed Sarkel and our people had to flee to a new homeland. But wait, my brother will tell you this part of our tale so I can take my evening meal.

#

CHAPTER THREE

———— ✝ ————

My Brother, Marót, Our Khazar Prince Saving the Kagan of the Khazars from the Dark Belly of a Viking Ship.

There's my brother, Marót: the kid with the two long brown-black braids. It's now his turn to tell you what happened when we came flying out of the cave's time tunnel and awoke suddenly in a blinding flash of light, and war, near our white fortress at Sarkel in Khazaria. Go on, brother.

Tell the time traveler from a distant land what you were up to when we landed at Sarkel a hundred summers into our future by going into that mystic cave in the Kafkas. Marót! Don't be shy. There's nothing to be gained staring at your boots my fine, smart, and handsome brother. Our guests are waiting to hear you. Show all your famous hospitality. And brother continued in our oral tradition.

Marót's Tale

I'm only Marót, a thirteen-year old boy who should have been at his own conversion today to the new faith. Instead, I watched through open shutters from where I hid in the rat-infested salt fish room beneath the mews and falcon's copse. I watched from above, as my youthful father, Bihar, Prince of the Bikhar Khazari, son of the Kagan, writhed in the sour blackness of the Viking ship's belly.

There, the Rus Prince Svyatoslav of Kiev had chained him. Olive oil from tankards dripped slowly into his eyes and ran down his arms. It streaked the blood as he kicked against the manacles that held him steadfast to the rolling long ship.

I saw Svyatoslav's men minting our own Khazar silver coins, our yarmaqs, as we call the coins in our Turkic language. The rabbis from Baghdad and Prague call them dirhams in Arabic. Father found that the Kievan prince minted Khazar coinage based on the known world's standards governing weights and measures of our times. So

Svyatoslav chained my father in the darkest hold of this Viking ship.

Another beating had spared my father's life for today. His guard from Kiev laughed at him, mocking as he crashed a bucket of water across the floor boards.

"What are you complaining about? You're a Khazar, not a Sabartu-Asfalu (an Oghuz Turk). We told you that you'd earn money working out. Instead, you're protecting barbarous refugees fleeing into our lands like thirsty rats."

"More often, I'm protecting them in their own lands. Where are my wife and son?"

"The Khatun of the Khazari?" The guard again laughed. "Now what business would we have in Kiev with your wife?" He waved his torch before my father's eyes.

"But if she were blind, what need would she have of eyes to share the captain's table? Now your son, that's another matter. You will tell us where you have hidden your son. Is he with the isinglass merchants?

"Where would a barbarous Khazar boy be— in rapport with the wild Karelians? Or perhaps he has been sent to Abkhazia?"

Bihar struggled in pain, filling his lungs with the dark mold that steamed the air. My father didn't scream out. Instead, Bihar listened to the squealing rats fighting in the darkness. His guard let fly the plug of musty water from a public slop bucket, and it slimed the Prince with fish guts, blood, and seaweed.

Before he left Bihar in darkness, the guard dipped his torch made of twisted reeds in pitch and waved the burning smoke in Bihar's face, forcing him to crawl even lower in the black space as the smoke burned his nostrils. "Are you an animal or a man, Bihar of the Kosarin? Do I see a wolf's tail on you? By the bite of the wolf you were born, and like the werewolf you are, you shall die slowly here, very slowly, unless you tell me where I can find your son, Marót."

The cold dampness allowed him to think. Did Prince Svyatoslav of Kiev want the Vikings and their allies, the Slav and Byzantine merchants to do away with the entire Khazar royal family? Or did he only want them exiled to the empty deserts of Khwarizm along the Silk Road? Bihar refused to struggle and contained his fury as Svyatoslav seized his chains from the guard's fists.

"Tell me again about the day your whole country turned Jewish."

"That day our King found nothing in Christianity or Islam that denied anything in Judaism. His decision was based on pure logic. Christianity can exist without Islam and Islam can exist without Christianity, but take away everything that has been added by Christianity and Islam to each religion and what do you have left as a foundation? You have Judaism."

"I'm a Pagan, and I'll always be a Pagan," Svyatoslav scowled. "I have nothing against Khazaria. I simply love to fight. When I'm not fighting you, I'm fighting the Pechenegs on my northern borders. I warn you, Bihar. Someday my people will gather the whole Byzantine Empire against you. When you were as Pagan as I, long before your nation turned Jewish, your daughters married the Byzantine Emperors. As soon as you decided to take up Judaism, Byzantium turned against you, and suddenly they see you sprouting horns. Where are your allies, now?"

"Olga, rules Kiev, not you," Bihar answered. "Your mother is a compassionate queen. You are too restless a warrior to be a spiritual ruler. Soldiers of fortune don't make good rulers. They're good only in carrying out orders, not leading men. You need to be at the core of the action to feel alive. And look at you—such a warrior she reared, a Christian Queen of Kiev and her Pagan prince son."

"Don't analyze me, Bihar of Balanjar. Your own destruction will come from those like Olga when her followers ally with Byzantium, not from my tolerant Pagan world." Svyatoslav shouted.

"Better watch your back, Prince Svyatoslav. Else your skull will serve as a drinking cup for the starving Pechenegs you slaughter."

Svyatoslav grinned. "No, go on, Bihar of Balanjar. Why did your whole country turn Jewish in one day? I must hear that story again, especially from a Bikhar Khazar. What would happen if the Pechenegs gave up their Pagan worship?"

"It's simply that long ago our Kagan Bulan could not find any other religion that denied the fact that our Creator gave the commandments to Moses on Mount Sinai who gave the law to six hundred thousand people."

Prince Svyatoslav scowled at the Khazari Prince as he moved slowly with an oil lamp and a torch, watching closely Bihar's wrist manacles.

"The Kagan is dead. Bihar, you are now King of the Khazari...King of the Jews. How does it feel to be one day a Turkic tribe in the steppes praying to a white horse--and the next, your whole country turns Jewish because your king declares you are the lost tribe of Simeon?"

The bald Kievan prince, mustache drooping, sat across the room as his torch flickered in the silence of the dark. Before the king of the

Khazari, the floor rippled with stripes of shadow. Svyatoslav shattered the torchlight into motion by waving fans that appeared to arch and stretch.

"Tell me, Turkic werewolf, why did your whole country turn Jewish in one day? Speak to me in my Kievan tongue. Or can you only say kusu kalkmaz? Have I have clipped your wings, my bird, o' nightingale of the Caspian? What right do you have to claim Jerusalem? Were all your battles fought to buffer my Kiev between Christendom and Islam? Why have you tried to halt my isinglass trade in the Kavkaz? Tell me why you sabotaged my right to the minerals of Khazaria?"

Svyatoslav felt Bihar's large black eyes on him as he watched the young Khazar struggle to sit up, gasping against the weight of his shackles. "The day my whole country turned Jewish--Bulan, Kagan of the Khazari, told his ambassadors from the lands of Christendom and of Islam that he had decided to accept Judaism because the Jewish religion is the oldest, and Christianity and Islam both sprang from it.

My Kagan's ancestor, Bulan, saw a great golden tree with branches. He wanted the roots of the tree and the trunk to be his foundation because the trunk and roots are the strongest and oldest part of the tree. 'If Judaism is the roots and trunk of the tree,' he declared, then why do you consider the branches?'"

"So the day my Khazaria, turned Jewish, we all took the roots that grew deep in established tradition. We chose the trunk that grew to the clouds, the oldest of the three religions presented to us. And from that day forward, my whole country remained Jewish."

"There were people of other faiths in your land," Svyatoslav insisted.

"Yes, but they always were free to choose whom they worshipped. And we came from many places here."Bihar leaned forward seeking to span a more distant arc. His eyelids fluttered.

"I saw your people carve totem poles," Svyatoslav shouted. "Werewolf! Sorcerer!"

"We didn't have carved idols of our own. We had tamgas, charms and talismans that we wore. What about those?" Bihar pointed to another tribe's standard, a Pecheneg's totem pole that the Vikings had propped against the ship's wall. It was decked with horse tails, tassels, silver mirrors, and Tengri-worshipped talismans.

"Our people didn't carry statues along the Silk Road," Bihar said anxiously. "We are not idolaters. Behold our fine orchards and homes. Do you see us living in yurts and leather-covered wagons?"

"Yet you do bring out a white horse for Tengri, for extra luck," said Svyatoslav. "We know you have been settled here for many generations."

"What about you, Svyatoslav? I hear your mother had herself baptized, but you refused and ran away. Why? If you're a secret Pagan, why are you allied with Byzantium? For your mother's sake? To inherit more than a throne? Do you want to learn from us how we bring down a Kagan by making him a figurehead and appointing a Bek and the Tarkhans to command our armies? Do you want one of these men to baptize you? Perhaps you want *my* faith other faiths beyond the mountains, or need to speak with an Imam?

Why is it important to you that we have accepted the Jewish faith? If you choose your own road, what do you want from the Khazar people?"

"To judge you, Bihar of Balanjar. We will try your Kagan Bulan's strategy in reverse. I've brought one Christian, one Moslem, and one Jew to judge you," Svyatoslav chided. The three blackrobed men stepped out of the darkness into the flickering light of the ship's belly.

"I am but one of three," each dignitary announced as he stepped into the light, "a Christian, a Moslem, and a Jew."

"Which faith will you choose for your people, Bihar? When will you announce your decision? Which one of the three men here will you choose to convert you to his belief?"

"What's your purpose in this game--to dishonor yourself?" Bihar asked.

"I want to hear about the day your whole country turned Jewish. It wasn't like that in my land." Svyatoslav ran his hand along the scar on his own cheek.

Bihar winced, but held the Kievan prince's gaze. "I've told everyone many times that rabbi Ha-Sangari of Byzantium long ago converted those who chose to Judaism. Now it's my turn. I hear that in Constantinople, my people, the Khazari are forced into conversion and made to choose between living next to a leper colony or being baptized. Perhaps the world didn't know we baptize daily in our mikvah.

"We are reborn again each day through the spiritual experience of bathing in our natural water mikvah. The Byzantines learned about baptism first from us—the Khazari of the tribe of Simeon, of the steppes and mountains, and most likely married to women from the Jewish communities of Persia that are merging with other Jewish communities. As soon as the attitudes worsen for us, we merge more tightly with communities as far away as Prague, Toledo, and Baghdad. "

"Forced conversion?" Svaytoslav mischievously arched one bushy eyebrow.

"No. Under Khazar rule for all who wanted to be converted, the people chose, not the King. We have many here in the lands of Khazaria, and they come from your land as well as many other lands."

"That is why they will choose again, Kagan. What will you choose, Bihar, now that you're King of a land that has been laid waste as the land of the Hittites was, and like an Egyptian pharaoh once declared, his peoples are no more?"

The Christian ambassador, a Byzantine priest entered. "Choose Christendom because we are based on faith."

"And where did your faith come from?" Bihar asked.

"From Judaism," the priest replied.

"I want a religion based on action and charity, not only faith." Bihar turned his head. The Moslem Imam stepped forward. "Choose the last of the faiths, Islam, based on one creator."

"From where did your faith arrive?" Bihar asked again. "I already worship one creator."

"From the oldest—when our Prophet visited the Jews of Medina."

"And what happened to the Jews of Medina?" Bihar gasped. "I will choose for myself and those who live in Khazaria one faith, and those who want to join it will be converted with me. The king and court has taken one of the three faiths. This is how it has been since the days of Bulan. I'm only doing the same as my ancestor, King Bulan has done long ago."

"Oh, not so long ago," the Kievan added.

"What did you decide?"

"My ancestors had to be convinced. Since both the Christian and Moslem religions come from the Jewish religion, it must be the oldest faith in one creator. The books of all three contain names and places that come from the oldest book.

"Therefore, my ancestors converted to the oldest religion in which the others are rooted. I will join the tree at its source rather than hang from the branches and shift with the winds. After all, it's a decision based on whether to imitate successful giants of the past or make a visionary leap into changing and stormy waters."

"Quite logical—to choose a religion that takes action and is not merely based on faith," Svyatoslav reasoned with his captive. He motioned to the three ambassadors of three faiths, and they were quickly taken up from the belly of the ship by guards.

"What do you want of my wife and son?" Bihar glowered defiantly at Svyatoslav. Without replying, Svyatoslav grabbed the oil lamp and the torch and signaled to the guard. His falcon was brought to him. Svyatoslav pulled on the heavy leather left-hand gauntlet and held the falcon by its jesses.

He threaded the narrow, black tethers through their openings, looping the tethers around my father's manacles, moving the hooded bird from his hand to Bihar's. Svyatoslav scowled with his wicked mouth, whipped off the falcon's hood blinders, and released it next to my father.

Svyatoslav left the Khazar King chained, thirsting and starving in the blackness, alone with the rats and the falcon.

"Turkic werewolf, here's your dinner," Svyatoslav echoed. "As a Pagan, what need have I of you with my allies in Byzantium or in Kiev for a King who takes the faith of the captives of Babylon?"

"And how many brides of Khazaria have Byzantium taken these days or sold to the Sultan of Baghdad in his wars against my people?" Bihar spoke loudly, but Svyatoslav had vanished with his three ambassadors.

Long after Svyatoslav and the guards left, I crawled from the trunk and found my father in the blackest reaches of the ship's belly. No one noticed that I had disguised myself as a cabin boy from Kiev.

"My father," I called. Bihar heard my voice.

"It's your son, Marót."

We hugged. "Where's your mother?"

"She's safe. It's a servant girl from Antioch who sits in her place and clothing at the captain's table. She will don her own clothes and depart with her people at the next port."

I helped him cut the manacles with the tools that I hid under my clothing and head covering. "You have heard about the Kagan?"

"Yes," Bihar groaned. "Was it the Kievan prince who murdered my father and made me King without a country?"

"No. His new horse threw him against a rock and over a cliff." Both of us held hands and jumped from the ship in the darkness of night. The only sounds made were the slaps of water on flotsam rafts of wood and the paddle of the oars. The long ship remained anchored in port.

"Where are we?" Bihar asked.

"Anchored somewhere between the Dnieper River and the coast of the Pontus. It's not far from old Chorpan's fishing village. See that road to the right? It winds uphill. We have a long journey before we reach Kiev. Once we leave the banks of the river, no telling what can happen."

"Chorpan's father is of the Chechen peoples," my father said. "His mother is a Kievan Jew, so everyone here addresses him now as the old Kievan Jew. He's of the lam, the mountain, as he says in his Chechen words. I know Chorpan will help us."

"I hope he has some dry garments."

"My old tutor spent so many years in my Khazaria, that he has taken the Jewish faith of his mother. Chorpan taught me his Chechen Zikr dance—the dance where the men jump over a stick held shoulder high. If only the Kievan prince understood how many different peoples have come to this land from so many places. Even the Kievan

Jews have moved here from Byzantium, Prague, Bavaria, Persia, Cordoba, and Alsace. And some came from Baghdad, Alexandria, or Haleb."

Our robes rustled as we kept our faces pressed against the wood and stared at the star-wracked sky. "They won't see us," Bihar told me. "We must find a way to disguise ourselves as Kievans and get back to Atil or Sarkel quickly."

My teeth ached with the cold of the salt water. Down and up we tossed, father and son, bobbing in a cold well of sanity before we were thrown back on shore like two pieces of flotsam.

Chorpan is beyond on the shore. "There's his signal," I told my father. "Chorpan would never leave us."

"Welcome to Little Khazaria outside of Khazaria," a gravely voice sung. It was old Chorpan, now a Kievan Jew--father's tutor and mine. I grinned impishly from ear to ear. Soon we would be home for a short time before we were forced to flee our homeland. On what adventures would my father, the new King without a country, lead me next in this tinderbox, my Khazaria?

I stepped cautiously out of the water, and we began to walk, or rather stumble toward a village with vicious dogs snapping at our heels. Father and I gulped lungfuls of sea air. We covered about two hours of walking that night towards the home of old Chorpan, or rather a house of logs and skins.

Chorpan's gaze sharpened. "We have many Khazari here, but I want to go home with you, to Atil before mayhem descends on our fortress at Sarkel—or are we too late?"

Horizontal rain lashed our faces like a thousand thongs. The quiet village was carpeted with cloudwhipped birch trees.

Farmers scythed their crop and burnt it, turning the air a teal blue. Judaized Khazar soldiers who fled along the Don River valley and beyond to the Silk Road are still showing us how humane and decent they can be. One of them even came back in the battle to lead the collapsing litter bearers who had joined those of two Byzantine Fathers of the monastery hospice.

The soldiers had a sorrowful expression. War spread throughout Kiev like a plague. The battle between Khazari and the Kievan Princes spilled over from Khazaria into the Kievan principalities.

"Has my daughter married yet?" Bihar asked in amazement. "I would have wished her to marry in Sarkel or Atil, if there were peace in my homeland."

"Hurry and you will arrive in time for her wedding."

Chorpan led us over the rough path of cobble stones that blistered our feet under soft-soled boots. "She has earned the right to marry in any place she wants."

At fifteen, my sister, Raziet-Serakh is going to marry Yusuf ibn Jacob, a cousin of Ibrahim ibn Jacob, the author of the first extensive account about Polin (Poland). This summer of 965 in the Kievan's year, Ibrahim ibn Jacob and his cousin

Yusuf made a trade and diplomatic journey from their native Toledo in Moslem Spain to the Holy Roman Empire and Slavonic countries.

Yusuf settled in Polin, where he told us a home awaited all of us, if we wanted. He came to Kiev to be married to my sister. Ibrahim told me he will return to Spain after the wedding when Yusuf will make up his mind if he wants to take my sister to Polin or remain in our Khazaria, or even go to Jerusalem.

Yusuf also asked all of us to go with him. All we wanted was to be in Sarkel where there were people from many different lands or in Atil where many spoke the Khazar language in the streets and Hebrew in the places of prayer.

Goat-skinned drums, finger zills, and shepherd's pipes pealed through the long house. The bride almost was afraid to wear the Tuva silk that the rebellious rabbi from Khwarizm smuggled into this small village of Khazari Jews beached between Kiev and the ports of the Pontus. And as a hollow sound ravaged the rooms, the princess, Raziet-Serakh of Atil, paused by a window.

Beneath a damask scarf, she covered her braided dark ash brown hair. Each of the Khazar nobles at the wedding gave Raziet-Serakh the prostration. They bended on one knee with the other leg stretched out sideways with their right arm in a clenched fist pointing to their left chest as a salute with head bowed. A line dance began.

A ribbon of Khazar males dressed as soldiers walked on bended knee with their right arm, fist clenched, to their chest. The men saluted outward and back as they moved, crouched down, in a straight line down the wedding aisle. Each of the men's left leg squatted in a deep knee bend, while their right leg jutted out forward as they inched down the aisle toward the bridal throne, moving slowly to the musical rhythms of flute, nye, harp, and hand drum. The line dance halted at the foot of the bride and groom.

My sister, Raziet-Serakh, a whippet-wiry bride, might have stepped down from a fresco with her Assyrian profile defended by the blazing topaz eyes of a lioness. Behind the window's shadowed lattice she gazed outside through narrowed lids at the crowd gathered to watch the final scene in a brilliant drama.

At noon the warm sun silvered the birches that rustled through the street. The birds screamed. Someone was screaming. The sounds ripped through the streets as the wedding music played louder.

Was that a human voice? Raziet-Serakh thought. Its sound was a compelling tattoo, muffled and strange, as if it belonged to a wounded beast. Panicky, shallow gasps were all she could manage.

The storm of emotions that overtook her sent her trembling. A day of wrath dawned at her wedding site. For just beyond the dark forbidding walls that reminded her of the towering fortress of Sarkel that guarded the Kagan's Judaizing for more than two hundred years, an Auto da Fe began, the burning of Pechenegs in the still largely Pagan village between Kiev and Atil.

The great crowd that was to come to her wedding instead gathered to watch the final scene in a drama more brilliant than the wedding of Raziet-Serakh, a princess of the Khazari. As the spectators formed a circle, the soft, seductive slapping of unseen hands sounded an obliging tattoo that prepared for the final crescendo.

A Pecheneg prince everyone knew came forward clad in Svyatoslav's garb of shame. Haggard and pale as whey from his long confinement in the dungeons, a young man the crowd called Jelek Khan stepped forward donned in the garb of the mythical hawk of Togrul.

There, in the same place in which the blood bath of other steppe people had begun, at the same time when the Kagan's family went into sworn secrecy, the twenty-year old Jelek ran his fingers through his thick, dark hair and roared with condemnations.

"Throw more wood on the fire, you jackasses! I'm paying the bill."

"Let him burn slowly with the other Pechenegs. Don't put any more wood on," came a reply from the crowd. "Why should it be over quickly?" The prince's strong face contorted like rubber as the columns of smoke rose.

"He's sprouting horns like a Sabartu-Asfalu!" A woman shouted. "The steppe's demons are escaping!"

She screamed and thrust a tamga of an iron horse against his lips. Jalek turned his head away. Once more he raked the eyes of the crowd at his feet and saw that the women's tears were sincere.

They begged, and pleaded, and prayed for him to kiss the talisman before he was burned. They even tore their clothes.

"I have been a source of profit to Svyatoslav!" Jalek saluted the crowd in the manner of an ancient gladiator. "How much did the sale of my home bring?"

Among the onlookers at his immolation were members of his own family, their presence there compelled by the Pagan Kievan prince. The executioner asked him again if he would kiss the tamga. Finally he did to avoid the pain of being burned alive. Jalek was quickly garroted and his body burned by a group of the still Pagan Kievans at the standards and totems of their enemies, the Pagan Pechenegs.

"The wedding has been postponed," Bihar protested in distress. Two serving girls nudged each other, exchanging meaningful wide-eyed stares, and then hurried through the dank, echoing rooms.

"I will not have my daughter married in fear," my father shouted. The scene outside grew into a raging mob, waving sticks. Bihar and I and closed the shutters.

"I will get word to Yusuf. Get out of your wedding dress," Bihar ordered. My father would not play the fool to the Kievan princes. We had to get the family back to Atil.

The smaller tables were lavishly set with an abundance of roast hens served in glazed earthenware casseroles. Servants continually replenished overflowing swan-bowls of magnificent fruits that arrived with the rabbi. Oil lamps burned, flattering the oddly placed royal blue drapes that hung against the weathered walls of skins and logs at Chorpan's house.

Outside modesty did not reveal what inside proved to be arched recesses cluttered with faded tapestries brought out of Atil. Two serving girls frowned, rolled their eyes at each other and nudged elbows. "I'm sorry, the wedding has been postponed." In a staccato burst of thunder, a powerful patron protested loudly to the servants. "Take back the presents!"

Father found a dry pair of boots that fit. The rancor of his new jackboots on the wooden steps and the tapping of his bronze-headed sword captured his audience. "Yusuf has fallen ill." He impaled his guests with a penetrating stare. In her room, Raziet-Serakh let her bridal dress slip to the Tabriz carpet. Outside, the crowd had not slackened, and the smoke from the charred posts and acrid odor of burning flesh were filtering intoher room.

Raziet-Serakh sat down before her silver mirror, and let out her braids. Today not only was my sister's wedding, but her fifteenth birthday. I helped her place her wedding presents in a wooden chest. A door hidden behind the shadowed lattice opened from the inside. Her heart rolled over. "I had to come this way," Yusuf said.

My sister was relieved to see him. "You know what's going on down there," he added meditatively. Raziet-Serakh nodded. "As long as we stay here, we're traitors--traitors to our homeland," she said, her eyes clawing him like talons. "Look outside the window."

Yusuf gave Raziet-Serakh a baffled look. "I cannot lose my self. Will you go with me to a new place, Polin, or even Prague? We can return to my homeland in Toledo or Ibrahim's winter home in Cordoba where I can learn to be a healer like the Kagan. For heaven's sake, what is it in life that you value?" A black eyebrow arched mischievously into his forehead.

"I dreamed last night that half of Khazaria had fought a bloody battle over you."

"You ignore even my ultimatums about Khazaria as my homeland." At the same time she pleaded common sense, inwardly she knew Yusuf was a man who would risk anything for her. I heard the door opening, and mother walked in, safely hidden here for weeks for the wedding. "I'll send the servants away," she whispered. She signaled me to leave with her.

The light in Yusuf's eyes shone like bits of porcelain. She studied a tendril of black hair that fell across his tanned forehead and smoothed his high cheekbones with her long, delicate fingers. There was an ache in her throat as she thought that this would have been the day she was to wed. His deep-timbered voice was gentle.

The clikata, clikata, clikata of the horses over dusty village cobblestones nearly shook Raziet-Serakh senseless. She gazed at her father's depthless eyes, black as a new moon, and full of expectation as he watched her, the Khatun, and Yusuf. I sat crouched in the darkness, following with them to wherever destiny allowed. We were again one family together, for however short a time.

"Do not let the Kaffirs put a cloud on your good fortune or your marriage," Khatun told her daughter. "Put on your wedding gown," mother declared. "I will see to it that you and Yusuf are married this night."

"By whom?"

"The haham from Baghdad. He is here with me. I had to send him baskets of fish, eggs and olives."

"But what about the rabbi from Khwarizm?

"We need the haham to help us once we reach Atil."

The horses didn't stop anywhere. Our family drove on, out of the village of the Pagans, and towards the quay at the Sea of Pontus where the haham's ship was waiting to stretch its canvas and flee across the silver blackness of the open sea under a path of moonlight.

Through the misty streets the horses galloped in the dark of the night. Clikata, clikata, clikata. There were no stars to light the black satin night, only the moonlit troika that drove us far from a fortress home that no longer would be Khazari by the light of morning.

"There is enough wine and oil," Khatun said, brimming, with optimism. On the decks, a few scrawny chickens scattered out of sight. Some music winded through the wooden passageways and faded into nuances of delight. Father leaned his arms upon the slimy taffrail and openly wept.

"Fear is everywhere," Raziet-Serakh cried. "It's the Sea of Meotis to the east where we should be headed, not south. We are Khazari without a country."

"We are Jews without a country," Khatun said.

"When we were Khazari, we had an empire."

"We have the world as our country," my father added. "We can go anywhere, and we will be welcomed as healers."

Khatun caressed a large key which she wore around her neck on a thick gold chain. "This key still opens the door to my family's ancestral home in Atil, in the lands of Astrakhan. Perhaps we should have returned to our homeland in

Derbend. We're here now, and this key has been passed on from mother to daughter for more than two hundred years."

"And will always be," Raziet-Serakh replied. "Lest we forget who we are." She felt as if she were choking on her own words.

Yusuf nodded. "In Toledo and Cordoba, we have the same type of keys, but only go there if you want to be sent somewhere else."

"At this time you would have been taking your marriage vows under the chuppah. What better canopy could you choose to be married under than one that sails to a new world?"

Raziet-Serakh blushed all the way to the top of her wedding dress. We stood together on the ship's deck watching how the rain tore the clay pots of pink geraniums from the window ledges of the white houses.

Here I stood a thirteen-year old boy, wondering whether I should even be at my sister's wedding. Oh, but Raziet-Serakh had plans for me. She handed me a proper gift to present to the rabbi. And the Khatun, my mother, showed me my new dancing boots lined with fine lamb's wool. Now I felt included and no longer out of place at this wedding. Only a Khazar and a mountain man would worry about new dancing boots in the midst of a war.

"Teach me what to say, father," Raziet-Serakh pleaded. "How am I to conduct myself at the ceremony?"

"The haham, the enlightened one from Baghdad will speak with you soon."

"And what of the sailors and the other passengers in this ship?"

"No one will hear a sound. The haham's cabin will be locked."

"And the haham?"

"In masquerade as a Kievan baker."

Khatun had left nothing undone. The oil lamps were left burning.

Father took a tiny tear vial out of his waistcoat pocket and handed it to Raziet-Serakh. "According to the Psalms, your tears are supposed to fill this bottle." Raziet-Serakh hid the tear vial in the plaits of her chignon.

"The tear vial will be the sign that you are one of us," father told my sister. "Wherever you go, it is the signal between Khazari that you will remember the faith and that Khazaria lives in our memories forever, even though are commanded to forget what we were before we were Jews. We do this because from today forward, we Khazari will be Jewish.

"We will not forget our families and that there was once a Jewish Kingdom, an Empire that spanned an arc from the Sea of Pontus to the Sea of Meotis, and that our homeland where the Volga runs into the Sea of Meotis will be remembered. I give you this so you will always know who we are. Our purpose in becoming Jews is to teach the difference between torah and tumah."

"I want to stand by you as you take your wedding vows," father said. "Tonight the Erusin--the betrothal ceremony will take place as part of the ceremony under the Chuppah canopy. It will be followed by the Seder Nisuyin--the marriage ceremony with the blessing over the wine and the Sheva Berakhot--the Seven Benedictions."

My father put his arm around his daughter's shoulders and shunted her away from the taffrail as footsteps grew louder. When the other people had passed he hurried the Khatun and daughter to the rabbi's quarters.

The door of the moonlit cabin was triple locked. Heavy, black cloth covered the windows to shut out flickering torches and oil lamps from prying eyes. Yusuf stood in a corner. The dancing shadows and rippling patterns of the wind-worn shutters moved in patterns across his face. He bolted the wooden shutters and the lattices.

In the dark chamber, Raziet-Serakh lighted a small wick flame and sat before the silver mirror. The embroidery on my sister's wedding dress had silver threads that shone symbols of prayer, secret in their meaning and hidden to all but family members as to their tradition.

Words and Gestures in the Ritual:
The Hamah explained how Yusuf was to say his blessing, the Shema: Hear O' Israel, the Lord, thy G-d, the Lord is one--that he was to utter the name of the Lord, Adonai, and touch his fingertips to his eyelids, and the other prayers, blessings from

the magnificent synagogue in Baghdad about which he had heard so much and how he had brought books of great learning and many rabbis with him to all our synagogues in Atil.

"Under the circumstances, it's impossible to have a group of ten men here. We can't even have two witnesses other than the parents of the bride," Khatun explained.

"Where are Yusuf's parents and the rest of his family?" the Haham asked.

"In Toledo." Yusuf felt his fists bunching at his sides as all heads bowed and swayed.

A loud knock on the door startled the wedding party. "I'm here," said Yusuf's cousin,

Ibrahim ibn Jacob. "Luckily I found out in time what happened to you." He removed his cloak and stood next to Yusuf.

"After you marry my children, can you marry Bihar and I?" Mother spoke in a calm and determined manner.

"We had to take our vows to each other in the secrecy of our home many years ago when there was a war, and so we were never joined by a rabbi of the great synagogue in Baghdad. In Atil we had a large wedding, but it would be a mitzvah, a blessing to be married by such a learned rabbi as the haham."

"I'll marry you, then. Just follow along with this ritual and we'll include one more couple," the Haham laughed.

"I've performed many kitchen weddings in Baghdad and in Atil when Jewish refugees from Baghdad fled to Khazaria and married husbands from Spire and Prague who also came to Atil. I've married Jews in villages along the Silk Road from Tabriz to Cathay, but this is the first time I marry a Princess of the Khazari to a learned scholar from Toledo on an isinglass merchant's ship."

"Peace be upon you, haham." Raziet-Serakh smiled.

"I'm writing the Ketuba, the marriage contract," The rabbi, the haham, had smiling hazel eyes, wide at the corner and almond-shaped at the far ends. "Your Hebrew names must be carefully recorded on the contract," he said, taking up his scrimshawed pen.

"Will the hatan--the groom--come forward?" Yusuf stepped up.

"Have the bride and groom fasted all day today?"

"Yes," Yusuf answered. "My Kagan made the fast possible by chasing all the guests from the public wedding. When he saw the fate that befell the Pechenegs in the street, he knew the Khazari people would be next. The celebration inside could never continue."

"You can eat at the Chuppah after I marry you."

The Haham's eyes danced with mirth. He pushed his wild, silver hair back under his kippot and laughed on a wisp of a breath.

"I will now instruct you how to pray the Minha service before the wedding, according to the customs of the Khazari and Babylonian rite of the Jews of Baghdad," the haham said. He went through the tones and melodies, translating all the Hebrew words into Khazari, explaining the significance.

Uttering Words Of Tradition,
The Amida And The Vidui:

"Now the groom must say his special Amida of 'Ereb Yom Kippur' with the special confessional prayers called the 'Vidui while he is praying the 'Minha service with a Minyan, a quorum. We don't have ten men present for a quorum." Isaac, the haham slapped his palms against his temples.

"Have you gone to the Mikveh?" Khatun asked.

"The what?" Raziet-Serakh trembled.

"The Mikveh, the bride's ritual bath before the marriage ceremony," said the haham.

"If I were in Atil, I would have remembered," she said apologetically.

"I've already checked the eligibility for the marriage. Of course in Baghdad, Cordoba, Toledo, Ishkandaria, or even in Prague, Cologne, Alsace, or the Loire valley you would have had to post the banns before you two could wed."

"Please, rabbi, we're on the open sea." Yusuf extended his hand with impatience.

Sit her in a basket. We'll lower it into a natural body of water, the sea, and she'll have gone to the Mikveh." Khatun declared.

"It's cold and raining, mother." Raziet-Serakh begged.

"You can't get married without the ritual bath."

"We'll deal with that after we finish the words of tradition," the haham said.

"Both parents are Jewish." The haham whistled a long breath. Then he spoke quickly. "From what cities in Spain did your family flee to Khazaria, Yusuf?"

"Toledo. I came to Khazaria and then to Kiev with my cousin, Ibraham ibn Jacob to hire helpers to copy the Torah scrolls," Yusuf answered.

"I see by the papers that Yusuf and Raziet-Serakh have not been married before."

"You know that," my father insisted.

"An engagement is marked without the writing of the conditions of marriage," the haham remarked.

"The traditions of our Sepharadim are different in Spain-- another way in Prague, and still another in Byzantium, Baghdad, Tabriz, or in Cologne or Spire."

"Yusuf," Raziet-Serakh whispered, sure of herself and her rightful place in the rituals and links of all the generations she could visualize. "So we will go in history as the Jews of Khazaria, let every detail that must be written, then be written."

My sister turned her head slightly and took her father's arm as he led her a few steps to face Isaac, the haham. Yusuf came out of the darkness and stood next to my sister before the great haham, who was garbed in the clothing of a baker from Kiev. Beside him stood his cousin from Toledo, Ibrahim ibn Jacob.

"Yusuf!" the haham Isaac spoke in a deep, gravelly voice. "Son of Aaron ibn Jacob, what is your Hebrew name?"

"Yusuf," he answered. "I will keep the name of Yusuf, though I have much to learn of the Khazar people."

"Raziet-Serakh, princess of Khazaria and daughter of Bihar of Balanjar, Kagan of the Khazari who insists he is of the lost tribe of Simeon and Amyra, the Khatun of Atil, daughter of rabbi Solomon of Mashad in the land of Persia, what is your Hebrew name?

"Shoshanna" after my rose garden," Raziet-Serakh answered.

"Raziet-Serakh is your Khazar name. You will use your Hebrew name henceforth," said the haham. Welcome Amyra of Atil. I heard you took a Hebrew name too, even though your family in Persia has been Jewish for eons."

The Khatun stifled a smile. "I took two Hebrew names for good measure, my own and the name,

Amyra upon my husband's conversion and that of my children."

Raziet-Serakh spun around and nodded to her mother. Yusuf took Raziet-Serakh's hand.

"Now following the drinking of the glass of wine, the bridegroom breaks the glass in memory of the destruction of the Holy Temple in Jerusalem, which is supposed to conclude the ceremony," the haham Isaac explained.

"You know we can't break any glass in here. The noise would attract attention," Bihar said, holding up the exquisite crystal wine glass.

"Well, that's what we do in Baghdad and in Byzantium," Isaac said. "When we meet in Atil, I will be happy to help you renew your vows with the finest crystal goblets, but by that time, you could be celebrating your twentieth anniversary."

Mother kissed the bride's cheek and the groom's. And Yusuf kissed his mother-in-law's hand. They hugged the haham. Everybody kissed one another's cheek.

A hearty kasher meal of boiled fish and olives, baskets of fruit, mother's honey cake, spinach, eggs, and home-made wine filled the air with scents of home once more. Yusuf lowered the haham and his cousin Jacob through the trap door in the rabbi's quarters to his secret hiding place with the help of the Khazar ship's captain.

"These couples are now married," announced the haham, "in the name of the kingdom of Khazaria, the Baghdadi rite of the synagogues of Babylonia, and according to the laws and usage of all the Jewish people."

"I call upon you to establish a loyal and fruitful house amongst the people of Israel, fruitful in charity, wisdom, and compassion, indeed, and if it is willed, family," Isaac said.

He handed the ketuba, the marriage contract, to the bride. "I know you don't have a written marriage contract. So I'll write several to keep for you in Atil, Baghdad, Ishkandaria, and in Jerusalem where these records can be found in the largest synagogues. I have the feeling you will be traveling far in the near future as I will."

Isaac asked the family to have more patience as he recited the Seven Benedictions. "You've waited a lifetime for this," he said, as he gave the blessings. "Give thanks unto the Lord for He is good, for His mercy endures forever. May the sorrows depart from Israel and rejoicing increase among us."

The haham rabbi then poured more wine and cider and handed cups to the bride and bridegroom and then to the parents. He opened his arms and beckoned to the two couples.

"Would the bride remove all her jewelry before she steps under the Chuppah?"

The women took off their jewelry and dropped the pieces into a satin brocade sack. "There's room for four people, move closer," he added.

Words of the Marriage Ceremony Begin

Isaac began the actual ceremony with the words "Besiman Tob, sabrei maranan" followed by the blessing over the wine and the blessing of "Erusin--the betrothal, "Mekadesh Israel al yedei Chuppah vekidushin.

The words were foreign and unknown to everyone in the room except the haham who then handed the bride and groom some wine to drink.

Raziet-Serakh and Yusuf sipped first. Then mother and father drank from the cup.

"Do you accept to marry each other by your own free will?" the rabbi asked.

"Yes."

"Yes."

The ring was then taken from Yusuf and carefully examined by Isaac. "I will now say the 'Kiddishin.' This is a blessing after which the groom will place the ring on the right hand index finger of the bride as he recites these words.

"Repeat after me."

"Be thou betrothed unto me by this ring in accordance with the laws of Moses and Israel."

Issac first had Yusuf repeat after him each word in Hebrew--'*Harei at medudeshet li betabaat zo kedat Moshe ve Israel*,' and then again in Yusuf's Judeo-Arabic language spoken in his native Toledo.

The haham had to be sure Yusuf understood the meaning. He did the same for Raziet-Serakh in the Khazar dialect. Father had taught Isaac his language long ago.

"We've waited a lifetime for this miracle," my father said. He drew mother closer and put his arm around her waist, happy at the sight of her delicate Khazar beauty.

"You can present her with the ring," Isaac added. Yusuf took out of his pocket a blue velvet box and placed the ring in her open palm so she could cherish it.

At the same time mother took off her royal Khazar wedding ring with the sign of the menorah and handed it to father who slipped it back on her finger, renewing her marriage vows silently and smiling with content and serenity after sixteen seasons of marriage. I smiled warmly at my parents and wished my sister and her husband well.

The Ketubah, A Marriage Contract:

"I shall read the Ketubah." Isaac stepped away from under the Chuppah. He began to read the marriage contract. "Since we do not have two witnesses--the Edim-- to sign this contract, will the both parents sign after the names of the bride and groom?" Each couple signed as witnesses for one another.

"Where is the groom's hat?" Isaac asked. Yusuf eagerly turned and twisted, searching the room for his hat. He saw it on a chair and placed it on his head.

"Now that the marriage contract is signed, would you please step under the Chuppah which I have so cautiously set up in this room? These couples are now married," the haham said, looking at my sister and mother with their grooms--one renewing her vows after many years, the other starting a new life far for the first time outside of the Khazar Empire.

"Byzantium is no paradise for an immigrant Jew," said the rabbi haham. "Yet for more than two hundred seasons in Khazaria no office stood in watchful and angry judgment over the consciences of those who heed the laws of Sinai.

What waits for you at the gates of Atil, my Kagan? Pray for peace in Jerusalem."

Once off the isinglass merchant's ship near Atil, the wedding dances renewed our faith.

The Khazar wedding is danced. Even a war will not stop the dance. There is power in the dance of the steppes, of Central Asia, of the Turkic tribes not settled among their orchards and farms. A Khazar's roots is with one Turkic tribe who is settled among the family's orchards, and a Khazar is for the most part, is an observant Jew.

Joining in with the dance were the Karachay and the Balkarians and the Alani. All the peoples of the Caucasus joined in the dance to celebrate the joy of the wedding. Love is universal and is what drives the life force through the darkest energies of outer space so the life force eventually finds new homes where water, sky, earth, and foliage grow abundant.

Even the dance and the dialect have its own tones and textures. There is power in the nigun or song. The Khazar dance purified and bound together the soul and elevated it to great heights. When it was mingled with the teachings of torah, the Khazar dance became a way of being one with all. Yet Jews from many countries took refuge in Khazaria.

Bihar, Chorpan, and I walked into the home where Raziet-Serakh prepared for the second round of her wedding, the time to dance and feast for all the wedding guests, and a time to give charity. A Khazar has no greater love than to give charity and to ride his horse upside down or parallel to insure his invisibility to all and hopefully, his invincibility as well.

"Access to certain temples can be achieved only through song," father declared as he rushed in and hugged the bride and groom. My father carried in his daughter, the bride sitting on a bier as she tossed white flowers to the wedding party. Four bearded best men dressed in black also helped Bihar carry her toward the groom as they danced.

Her arms waved and clapped, but she cast her eyes down for the sake of modesty.

Raziet-Serakh sat and swayed as Bihar, Chorpan, and his sons carried Princess Raziet-Serakh toward the chuppah, looking like the flower for who she was named. Another four men brought the groom onstage. He danced with feet sliding, as if on ice skates, toward the bride. Then the four men carried the groom seated in a chair on their shoulders dancing three steps forward and two steps backwards.

They took two small steps to the left and two small steps to the right, raising their bent knees high, as if they were the baton twirler leading a march, swaying slowly toward the chuppah. It's a veiled or draped canopy under which the bride and groom will be united in matrimony by the rabbi.

We had a rabbi from Prague, one from Cologne, and one from Baghdad. Two Persian rabbis also walked in. It was as if the world's rabbis met in Kiev and brought with them so many rabbis from Khazaria's cities of Atil and Sarkel and Samandar that you couldn't fit them all into one big room.

We all danced a three-section song with the section repeated. The songs in a minor scale had a happy lilt. Music focused on of feelings of joy and enlightenment, spiraling in an ever-uplifting mood.

Yusuf danced three steps forward and two steps back, two to the side and three away then leaped toward the bride. The mother-in-law of a cousin of Jacob placed gold bracelets on the bride's arms with joyous peals of "my soul." She added, "My little bird, my little one."

A group of Khazar musicians encircled the bride and groom as they swayed back and forth on the shoulders of the dancers. In Atil the musicians played side by side with a troupe of Caucasus mountaineer musicians. But in Kiev, the goatskin drums of the Khazari beat out a one-and-uh, two-and-uh, rhythm. The rhythm arose, becoming louder.

Suddenly a low-pitched shepherd's pipe trilled notes in a shrill melody. A fiddler wailed into the purple-salmon sky. Then the musicians from Persia and Baghdad brought in their kanoun and nye to play Taksim in the style of Magham Seekah.

The Kievan Jews from Byzantium played the twangs of their strings. Their balalaikas strummed faster than the songs of played on a Baghdadi kanoun as the bride and groom dance around the chuppah, after being united in matrimony under it.

Thumping of the drums grows louder. Now in an Abkhazian leaping dance, and after, in a Russian chair. Lines of men danced the Kievan kazatchka with the groom, bending deeply the left knee, with the right leg extended outward in a line formation. The left arm is flung out horizontal, while the right arm is bent at the elbow and hugs the right hip. The men walked around the chuppah in what the Kievans call their kazatchka formation.

This dance was not always Kievan, but of the steppe, the Caucasus, and the Sea of Meotis--a sea that the Persians named Khazar. As the wedding dance to the music progressed, the music now changed to a major scale.

Each dance lasted up to a half-hour, until a new melody was introduced, and fresh dancers took their places. Everyone danced a new dance of the Jews of Bavaria called the *Rikkud* at Raziet-Serakh's wedding exactly as they danced it at the end of the Sabbath period.

I danced the Tish. The Bavarian Jews, new to our lands taught it to the visitors from Prague who showed it to us. It's a long, slow meditative melody swayed in a circle of men and a separate circle of women who never meet. The melody began as a song sung at the rabbi's table by the rabbi's son. The Tish is a nigun, or sacred song, but we Khazari made it danceable to wedding music. It has several parts, and the mood varies.

"Tell me about the Tish, father."

Bihar laughed at his dancing son. "Let the musicians tell."

And a musician came forward and played a refrain toward the end. Between sections, the women danced an "awolloch" pastoral melody, while the men swayed to the high notes of a shepherd's pipe. Both men and women danced to a slow, lengthy, introspective, soul-stirring song. We all danced with deep feeling and sung Khazari and Hebrew songs with the same emotion.

One rabbi from Tabriz began to lead all of us in a march as the bride and groom finally danced with each other, holding a scarf between them they danced and circled around one another. And so we danced, in a long line, out the door, down the village cobblestones, and danced and danced all the way back to Sarkel. The wedding party moved like a writhing dragon.

People made way for the wedding party and the music. The bride, groom, and everyone in the wedding party moved forward. The soldiers stood aside to let the wedding caravan pass. We danced slowly to the stirring wedding song, dancing our way home from Atil to what remained of the ruins of Sarkel.

From Atil to Sarkel
Sarkel, Khazaria—near Astrakhan in the Summer of 965 of the Common Era
I watched as my father, who only ascended his throne as Kagan this summer, dressed for my conversion in Sarkel as the spiritual leader that he was destined to be, but with no place to go and unsure of how many he would lead. My father raised his skullcap and stared through the tattered hat. His voice had a cold, slick quiver of revulsion.

"Blood on my hands," he told the wise rabbi who traveled all the way from Persia.

"Repairing the world," he whispered." Bihar's voice grew louder. "Put on your hats," he shouted disdainfully to heaven.

Folk tales of more than one hidden *Sefer Yezirah* scroll spread throughout Khazaria from the Sea of Pontus to the Don and on to the Caspian. One of the rabbis came to Khazaria from central Europe, near Prague. We had time-traveled with him from the future far into the sixteenth century near Prague, and back again to my time in the ninth and tenth, when we had the only Jewish kingdom in all of Russia and the lands up to Byzantium.

He offered Bihar copies of the *Sefer Yezirah* that revealed the formula for creating a Golem from clay. Bihar thought the Golem reflected chaos and unrest. The Kagan's search for the essence of the Golem concerned a rabbi out to protect his people from disaster by bringing to life a clay-sculptured figure that runs amok.

What if the Golem was unleashed to save Khazaria from destruction, instead? Bihar thought. What if Bihar, the healer and Kagan of the Khazari could ask the Golem to curb chaos in his lands? What if it didn't run amok like a monster as the folk tales revealed? Bihar rejected the Golem tale, and had the *Sefer Yezirah* copies secreted from our Khazaria. He sent copies with other rabbis leaving Sarkel. He was more concerned with the fate of Khazaria's Torah scrolls.

"None beneath the Kagan of the Khazari can take this Torah to Kiev," decreed the Persian rabbi, opening the ark to show Bihar sacred scrolls safely hidden in the walls above a chest of frayed skullcaps. "Yet I don't think you're going to Kiev. If I know you, you'll find your way to Jerusalem in the garb of what, this time, my Kagan? Another merchant selling isinglass where the Volga meets the Sea of Meotis, or an Imam from Khwarizm on a pilgrimage to Mecca by way of Jerusalem?"

Inside the shattered white fortress of the Khazari at Sarkel, by the Don River, the Kagan, Bihar began to daven to and fro, praying as the Persian rabbi guided a pointer at the letters Bihar long before had copied into his own language. He watched me as I gave my conversion speech inside. Outside, soldiers gathered.

The Rus soldiers took Bihar outside and let my father go. Each time he was stopped, someone would say, "Let the Khazari king do what he wants." He carried babies, newly born and laid back into his arms, dead. One with ice-blonde hair, but with glassy gray eyes and a small cut on the belly. Bihar kissed him and found a soldier to help him lay the baby on a bench.

Three minutes later, his five-year old brother, already stiffened, came to join him. The coppery smell of blood ripped through the forest. Bihar had opened a door to the brick fortress at Sarkel along the Don River that its Greek chief engineer, Petronas Kamateros, had built a century before when summoned by Bihar's great grandfather.

Now Bihar drew back in familiar horror: a pyramid of corpses lying amid the Kievan ruins. He closed the shattered door, and waited.

I saw that far to the south, Sarkel and Atil had fallen to Rus Prince Svyatoslav, and Bihar now found himself slamming the same words into people who passed by: He shouted to the Khatun (Queen), "The babies as well, wanted war, my friend?" She turned to a Kievan Rus soldier who shrugged. The soldiers had gone without sleep eight nights in order to destroy the Khazari fortress at Sarkel. Their ships came by sea in the night.

The chain-mail swathed Khazar horsemen in pointy helmets had settled the steppes by then and had great orchards, but the sea? To a Khazar, who boasts finer horsemanship than anyone, riding alongside the horse upside down, and invisible to weapons, it was not to their advantage to be attacked by sea.

Music of the *nye*, harp, and kanoun in the Persian style with the quarter tones of the Baghdad *taksim* nuances wafted from the children's room where the families of the rabbinical scholars from Persia and Baghdad came to teach the difference between torah and tumah. No war could stop the harps. I took up my fiddle and began to play at my own conversion. That day I realized I am a man, far beyond my thirteen seasons.

"Come on, for God's sake, there are seriously injured people here," Bihar cried.

The Khazar soldiers guided Bihar, at the risk of his life, as the war with Rus Prince Svyatoslav was at its peak. A Byzantine merchant, traders from Khwarizm (northwest Uzbekistan), Volga Bulgaria, Azerbaijan and Persia had perished.

Their inn was crushed by the prince's catapult, and in three vaulted rooms laid a dozen traveling merchants--wounded, burnt, their stomachs open, and their arms torn away. Bihar and some Khazar soldiers, the two Byzantine Fathers, and the Khatun all joined in, but they were not enough to carry the wounded across the alleys.

The remains of a fortress had attracted Prince Svyatoslav's warriors. I found myself hiding where the lazy golden flames flickered in the warmth of the summer sun.

Where I hid, shadows danced as I had danced at my sister's wedding or at my own conversion in the midst of a thousand carpets that the Rus soldiers of Prince Svyatoslav had gathered from Sarkel and sent to Kiev. We were left with only the woven reed mats.

Three visiting families bringing a new Torah scroll from Baghdad to Sarkel were wounded. A woman's arm had to be amputated and cauterized. All their faces were riddled with black-holed oil burns. They said nothing, not even a moan. But they kept their large black eyes wide.

The Turkic and Mountaineer allies of the Khazari came from the Caucasus Mountains like soft dragons face to face with the Rus silver bears sailing down the Don to many Black Sea ports.

The place of wooden synagogues, the Jewish quarter, stretched like a tough, earth-toned skin of stones. I prayed with the Mountain Jews. Persian-speaking Jews and the Mountain Jews from the Caucasus had built their synagogues facing west because from Persia, Jerusalem was located to the west.

Jews from Central Europe and the Rus lands who had arrived early in Khazaria built synagogues with windows facing south, toward the Eastern Mediterranean in the direction of Jerusalem, and they turned in that direction when praying. Prince Svyatoslav's warriors struck the holy places, the ruins, while the children of Khazari fought, cantillated, davened, and divined to and fro in prayer, and scattered in the streets.

The reflection of my father's face in the polished silver mirror of his standard revealed a tall, muscular young man of 34 years with the honey-colored complexion of one who spent his days riding in the sun. His curly short-clipped dark brown hair flowed in side curls, constrasting with the controlled braid in back that flowed from beneath his helmet over his right shoulder. Three bands of malachite beads bound the braid. Bihar's tense lips gave him a look of confusion.

He staggered in the distance to a ruined Byzantine monastery. "Am I in the right place?"

Bihar's voice held steady as he walked up to visiting Byzantine and Armenian priests standing far enough from their ruined church.

"Courage is not in the young people," the Father responded.

"Go out and pick up the wounded," the priest called to two young men.

"You're having a hard time getting people to do that," Bihar reassured him.

Raziet-Serakh, a woman from Baghdad, who had just given birth sat on the stairs with the baby in her lap, still attached to the cord. Bihar remembered her. He had bought ewes from her when she arrived in Khazaria before the prince waged his war. Her husband copied scrolls and bound special books for the children.

"Please take me back home," she begged Bihar.

"You have no home now," Bihar scowled over his shoulder.

"But where shall I go?" She cried.

"Over there." He pointed northwest to the grasslands of the steppe. The Rus soldiers asked him to do so.

Bihar carried her and I cradled her baby into the back of my father's donkey cart, and then he swooped up her little daughter who sat beside her.

"Idillah, idillah," she gasped, thanking him, taking his hand and calling it the hand of God. "Atil?" He asked. He thought she pointed the way to the Khazar city of Atil. "Atil is wasted," he said sadly.

"Idillah," she repeated in her own tongue. "Yes, idillah," at last he responded in her own language.

"I have learned Arabic long ago from rabbis in your great center of learning. When Baghdad is done with her wars against my people, I shall return there to study, speaking your tongue as well as any emir. From a priest in Damascus, I have learned Aramaic. And from those like you in my Khazaria, I have learned Hebrew. Who will light a candle in memory of my language, after tonight?"

Bihar retorted, narrowing his eyes. "What Mishnah will I write at Javneh for my people?"

She covered Bihar with blessings. He slowly drove the donkey cart toward the monastery that had a resting place open to all. A visiting Armenian priest provided from his own to help the villagers when the Byzantine priest's well ran dry.

The Rus prince's soldiers had destroyed all the Khazar places of sanctuary. At the end of the narrow, dark street a little boy was limping, his hands waving wildly. "Go away, get back!"

The Rus soldiers were shouting at him in languages he did not understand. Bihar stopped and leaped toward the boy who scratched at the slivers in his bare feet.

"Where is your mommy?" Bihar asked.

"Where do you come from?" The boy said and repeated with glassy eyes. "Where is mummy?"

He had lost his mind. Bihar carried him off to the monastery's room of hospice.

With his hand extended, Bihar stopped cold as he stared at its golden door knocker made in the image of a human hand.

"Hashem," Bihar whispered. "The hand of the Creator." Outside the monastery there was another cart. Bihar turned to look inside, thinking it was empty.

He jumped back. Five little children, one a baby of two weeks, lay there, as white as if they were made of alabaster, and covered with blood.

One by one Bihar took them out. They were put on the plank with their mother and covered up. They were those who had been left in the ruins, in order to take care of the wounded children who were still alive.

The father, arrested by soldiers, was unable to take his family further. Gently, Bihar picked up from the bottom of the cart a baby's sandal and put it in his pocket.

As soon as the rain stopped, nightingales by the dozens swarmed to pick grapes. Darkness fell like a fat snake in twenty coils amid the naked glory of a blizzard of stars.

The crescent moon rose over the deserted fortress at Sarkel. Bihar's donkey cart slid over a few feet between the mountains of the two halos, a snow-capped barren thing.

Bihar had returned to the monastery's sanctuary for the wounded.

A Rus soldier was still there, dead against the wall with an ax and a small rivulet of blood running from his head. The Khazari donkey carts with many family's possessions were slowly burning against the blackish red sky.

"Where will you go?" Asked an Armenian priest, who offered Bihar a plate of chickpeas and olives. "Your soldiers told me you perform miracles for your people. Maybe you should change your name to Nissim. In Hebrew it means miracles, he said. Your rabbi told me that. Why don't you eat?" He persisted. I'm Ter Manvelian."

"I can't," Bihar shuddered. "I can't stand the smell of my own hands."

The Father went down to the flagstones where three hundred Khazar refugees slept on the ground at the foot of a red lantern by the consecrated bread.

"Take this body for your sake." The Byzantine church service went on. "We share the church," the Armenian priest said. "The Greek in the morning, the Armenian in the afternoon."

"Are you sure I'm really in the right place?" Bihar asked. The Armenian priest touched him gently on the shoulder. "You're a Jew now, and so is he." The priest pointed to an icon.

Mothers taking refuge in the basement had no water to wash their babies. Children cried for food, and there was no more bread. The Father briefed the monks on what to say to Rus and Khazar soldiers. What do you say when two opposing sides fighting in a war have to share the same healing room day after day?

Suddenly a great healer entered the room. Bihar ran to meet him and thrust a document in front of the healer's face.

"What are you?" The healer asked, looking at Bihar's deeply-tanned face.

"I'm from Atil, now, a Jew. My great grandfather is from Alania. My sister and I were adopted by the Kagan of the Khazari. We were orphans from Alania. We became the Kagan's own beloved children."

"When you were Khazarian, you had a country, and you had the Sea of Meotis. Now that you're a Jew, you belong to the caravans of the Silk Road. You are from Alania. Where else would you go but the villages of your North Caucasus? Look, I have a friend in Abkhazia."

"I have a country," Bihar announced. "When I pray, what direction do I turn to, Constantinople or Jerusalem?"

"Take it easy. I'm Jewish myself, from Kiev."

"This order has the royal Rus seal," said the healer.

"Why do I need a Rus seal, if my grandfather is old and now I'm Kagan of the Khazari?" The order granted permission to bury the bodies that were piling up at the entrance of the monastery.

"We have no more carts or wagons," Bihar said. The heat of the next dawn brought the stench in waves, and the whole monastery had to burn all their incense in large gold lamps that swung on heavy chains from one end of the building to the other.

The priest did the hardest work. Bihar handed covers to him, walking in the blood with worms wriggling in it. I searched around to see what I could do to help him.

A Khazar tarkhan rode up, a commander with no one to lead.

"I'm coming to claim the body of Khatir, a dead Khazar."

"He's here," said the Armenian priest. "The rabbi will be taking him in a moment."

"His family paid to have him buried as a Jew," he added.

The tarkhan left with the rabbi and one body in a wagon. Bihar stopped the wagon. "Can't you give aid to anyone else?" The dead were piled up outside. "How many can you fit in this wagon?"

The rabbi said. Bihar watched the wagon driving away filled with occupants.

One by one, my father, the Kagan Bihar carried the bodies off. The limbs easily became detached from the bodies. Bihar carried once again the cart with the mother and her five children. Just as he was arriving with the people at a Jewish cemetery, the soldiers of the Rus prince rode up on their horses.

Prince Svyatoslav was there with his tall silver helmet on his head, and his Viking soldiers who sailed down the Volga in the great long ships. He didn't see the bodies. A long line of horsemen rode toward the burial fields.

Bihar swept off the cover from the bodies so Svyatoslav would take a look. The Khazari women saw it, and a Rus soldier shrank back.

"Cover it, cover it—and in the Jewish tradition, please!" a Khazar craftsman shouted, jumping between Bihar and the Rus prince. Bihar obeyed. Bihar and the rabbis entered the cemetery where a man was burying his wife and daughter. He strutted to the communal pit through the pestilential odor.

Bihar had passed over, one by one, the babies whose heads were opening up. "Baby sandals of blood," he muttered. "Would we be treated so in Jerusalem?"

I must get into the proper disguise and go there without haste, he thought. He stared through his hands. My father spent his thirty-fifth birthday burying our past, but who would light a candle in our people's memory?

"Do you think you can turn Jewish in a moment and then expect to be buried in Jerusalem?" The Rus prince shouted to Bihar. "I should first be in Jerusalem before you."

"Why? Is it important to you as a Pagan?" Bihar answered Svyatoslav.

"Certainly not to be baptized in the River Jordan," the prince groaned with a crooked grin.

"The war is not over for me as long as the Pechenegs fight, and for you?"

"You will absorb my people in the Crimea and in the Caucasus. Then you shall become us." Bihar replied. "I told you many times that we all come from the same place and will return to it—unless each person makes a war because he thinks he's different."

"In what way?" the Rus prince baited. "I hope not to look down on Kievans who are settling here."

"No, not to be a lion looking down at prey from the highest peak of the Kavkaz," my father answered. "Only to remember who we are now as our laws command us—that our mission is the *book*. What's your mission, Svyatoslav? The skull as a drinking cup?"

"To expose your coup d'etat as the real reason your whole country turned Jewish in a day. You can't fool me, Bihar. Your people made the Kagan a figurehead. That's why you have a Bek and a Kagan. One to govern and command your soldiers and the Kagan, a spiritual leader. I know how your people began to almost worship your Kagan—that their lives were bound by merely the existence of the Kagan. That's why you have reduced him to a rabbi, a teacher. Did your people start to worship him?"

"The tarkhan commands our soldiers," my father replied. "I told you we are now the people of the book and need a spiritual leader to teach us torah."

"A Kagan to teach what any rabbi from Baghdad can teach? How much did you pay to bring in spiritual teachers from Tabriz or Prague, Toledo, Alsace or Spire?"

"You must have been spying on us for many years to know from where our spiritual leaders are sought.....but you're mistaken....Our Kagan is from Atil, here in Khazaria."

"Kagan? There are no more Kagan of the Khazari….In a generation your princesses will be married to the Magyars."

"You're looking at a Kagan, Svyatoslav. We are not going to go away, and certainly not as part of the house of Israel. That surely has guaranteed our survival."

"Did it?" Svyatoslav declared. "Maybe I should use the word rabbi instead of Kagan. Don't you people know when you have been… assimilated?"

"I have corpses to bury," my father interrupted him. "So have you. Others will come after us that will challenge you far more than the Kagan of the Khazari. Without us, who will protect you from the wave coming?" Svyatoslav left deep in thought.

Later Bihar staggered out of the cemetery, past two Khazar women. "I am that I am," one told him. "So to whom do you belong?"

A line of Khazarian youths with side curls wearing the lamb's wool hats of the Mountain Men hurried to see what a Byzantine church looked like. They walked behind the donkey carts and fine steppe horses. The healers from Abkhazia and Chechnya taught them their warrior stick dance, the Zikr. When the Rus prince saw the dance, he forbade it forever.

"I'll never give up my Zikr dance," the Chechen healer told the Kievan and Abkhazian healers nearby. They all came, like wise men, drawn to war to heal or kneel. Bihar met Chorpan again. Old Chorpan had brought him itakh, puppies, when he was a boy.

"Come back with me to Kiev," Chorpan admonished the Kagan. "I have found a home for you in Polin—the place of rest where the king welcomes you."

"I'm not a merchant, Chorpan," my father told his old tutor. "I am a healer."

Father took out his little leather sack. "See these thin needles? I use them for healing. Along the Silk Road a great healer from Cathay, Li, willed them to me when I saved his life. He told me where to find his teacher. I had him brought to my court, and he taught me how to use the needles to heal.

"Let me show you how they work in the zones of energy. The healers of Cathay can work miracles if the needles are moved in circles along the correct pathways."

Father placed one of the thin needles at a point on his hand. Chorpan stared in amazement. "You must travel with me."

"Take your son on your travels," Chorpan answered. "But make me needles like that so I can take them back with me. I'll let you know whether they work....You must train others how to use them, or the secret will go out with you. In the wrong hands, those healing needles will be used as weapons."

"Any healer from Cathay can show you where the needles are placed for healing." Bihar felt comfortable with Chorpan, his regent and tutor for many years. "Where will I go? What will happen? I'm a Jew now. Nothing's the same. When I travel, people think I'm a Moslem from Persia on a pilgrimage."

"Who?"

"The Arabs. The Rus. The Byzantines. The Persians. The Turkic tribes."

"The Kagan is the last to know when the whole of Khazaria has been taken."

"Must I lose who I am? Is that the only recourse?"

"You have to belong to something," Chorpan said, slapping him on the back.

"Go, go along to help the others. In them you'll find out what side you belong on and where you are."

Near Sarkel a horse rolled into a ditch crushing new trees. A wagon driven by the son of a rich Persian merchant stopped.

"Are you headed for Kiev?" The young man said.

"Why are you riding in royal Khazar wagon?" Bihar asked.

"It's a Rus wagon now."

"That's my son's wagon."

There was no room in the wagon, so I had to go with a merchant who knew where my mother, the Khatun remained in hiding.

I crawled under a blanket in the wagon. "It's all right, father. The merchant is taking me away from this place." The Queen peered out from under a canopy. "We're going to stay with my sister in Kiev. A family of Jews from Prague married into another from Cologne. They came to Kiev to find a bride for their son."

Bihar nodded. "I'll send for you."

At the last moment, I jumped from my mother's wagon full of women and children and followed my father. The cart was full, but I squeezed my thin, gawky frame between two others and groaned as I eased myself upright.

The wagon stopped in front of a burned-out village bakery. Rus soldiers looted loaves of bread and urns of pickled eggs.

"Stop it," cried the Armenian and Byzantine priests.

"Rabbi, rabbi, the priest called out. "Order this place closed."

The rabbi from Baghdad had the shop closed.

Bihar and I went on the road again. Nothing makes a boy grow up faster than travel. The royal wagon passed a dead woman lying in a ditch.

"We're not going to Kiev," Bihar said.

"Proceed west."

"Why?" Chorpan asked.

"Because I'm in disguise as a pilgrim on my way to Jerusalem to deliver special Torah scrolls and also make a living along the way with these fine healing needles from Cathay. I also have people I trust who have made a place for me in Polin. No one in Polin knows I'm Jewish. The Rus are ordering all Khazari to return to Kiev. Whom do the Rus fear most? Not the Khazari, not the Turkic tribes, not the famine in the land of the Mongols, not their brothers in Byzantium, not Rome, but the sword of Islam. Where do I stand as Kagan of the Khazari?

"If not for me, the entire world would have one religion, and guess what that one religion would be? Where shall I stand without a land? It is we, the Khazari, who freed the Kievan prince's people from war and famine. And how does he thank us? By destroying Khazaria."

"People covet their neighbor's herd when their own bread basket is full," Chorpan wailed sadly in a minor key. He strummed the strings of his chunguri to the clickata of his horse's steps.

Soldiers of Prince Svyatoslav rode in front of the Khazari caravan, arrows pointing toward them and their cities. Voices blared across the steppes while wild horses whined.

"You must leave now for Kiev or go back where you came from. If you don't, your houses will be destroyed."

"Go back where? Do you see us living in yurts or homes? We are many from different places," Bihar told the soldiers. "Khazaria is not only a seasonal grazing field for wandering Turkic tribes. It's a state of mind. Jewish refugees from Byzantium, Persia, Mesopotamia, and all the lands of Europe have flooded into our realm for at least the past two hundred years.

"These refugees gave us their Hebrew heritage. Send us to Jerusalem. In what direction do you turn when you pray?"

Bihar jumped out of his wagon. "Where are you going to send them, back to? Could it be Baghdad? What about those from Constantinople or Kiev?"

A dead woman carrying two loaves of bread lay in the same ditch for two days. Bihar dug a hole under a rock and buried her with the bread.

"Go find two rabbis," Bihar shouted to Chorpan. "Go!" He repeated. A burial party was quickly formed. Bihar prayed with them, according to ritual.

In the Armenian priest's monastery, Bihar passed by two wounded children who had gone mad. A Jewish healer came in leaving his weapons of war outside.

"What are you doing?" Bihar asked, watching the healer work.

"Pinning a name to each of the wounded because Prince Svyatoslav's soldiers are coming."

The priest nodded to the healer, then quickly pulled Bihar aside.

"You're in a monastery of healers and priests from Armenia who are here to meet with the Byzantine monks in their outpost. During this war their healers saved hundreds of Khazari Jews by hiding them. It's not good for Prince Svyatoslav's men to come here. You must help us Armenians help your people."

Bihar carried back the wounded from the villages to the monastery. Horses ran wild, and most of the carts and wagons were stolen. Soldiers from both sides lay unburied in the wheat fields.

Bihar's mind went back to another war in which he fought as an ally, in the Caucasus. The people he had been hiding out with, the Adyghe, Shopsugs, and Abkhazian Mountain Men were accused of welcoming the Imams of Islam as liberators from the threat of the Slavic princes.

Svyatoslav was ruthless in hunting down the collaborators who had welcomed Bihar posing as a fellow Moslem from the Sea of Meotis. The dead looked the same as those on the steppes of the Caucasus.

"I've played pilgrim in disguise too long. I have to take a side. Now that my son also has accepted the Jewish faith, I can't risk staying a King of a thousand disguises any longer," Bihar chided Chorpan.

The next day a tense and tedious grey tone rose inside Bihar like a madhouse. Back in his makeshift dwelling, camped on a field of dry grass, he checked his weapons see whether they were ready for battle. His contact from Atil was the Khazar tarkhan, Baghatur, whose name meant brave warrior. Bihar's last hope, his infinity of mirrors, his new leader, must live.

He was a rubber stamp in the hands of his rulers. Baghatur watched two cockroaches running across the lush Persian carpet. "Books don't break. Books are better than people," he told Bihar.

A cool breeze from the shadowed lattice rushed over his wet body. On the horizon a taupe slit swallowed a blue bay of battle tents. In the distance, Bihar watched the flickering torch light above the gates of one home below.

He saw the carvings and wondered whether the crescent above the door stood for Islam or the old Moabite moon god that came from Ur? The old crescent represented the downward curves of the Tree of Life. He had the same Cow symbol on the doors of his boyhood palace at Sarkel.

Baghatur's crude leather and bone weapon again jutted from the shadowed lattice. Between openings in the encampments, his would-be leader could be seen addressing a crowd of people. He was standing in his wagon with unseen tears in his eyes, giving a speech of hope and reclamation for this people, promising more free education, more free medical care, and Baghatur's hand-carved Meotis weapon aimed at the potential assassin of the future leader of the Khazari in exile.

"Give me a better reason for this," Bihar whispered. Baghatur remained silent; only his green-gold eyes were alive. Below a circle of young mothers cradled their babies. One was an assassin. The young mothers, arriving veiled in a caravan from Baghdad, wore the black djellaba.

Male relatives escorted them. The women chatted on high key and laughed merrily in the air, straightening their babies' swaddling. Only one wasn't only a young mother. One was an assassin in disguise, but which one? Bihar wondered.

One mother had smiled for the past half-hour, rocking her one-year old son, while her nine-month pregnant belly bobbed up and down to the rocking cradle and staccato chatting. She held a rattle in one hand and had stopped the rocking cradle to flatten her hood with the other as the wild arrow from Baghatur's Chinese bow hit her clean through the navel.

The young woman of eighteen whirled about suddenly by the impact as neighbors swirled their heads about. "The poison she holds for our new leader will never leave her cloak," Baghatur whispered. Bihar heard only the rustling of dry branches in the wind. The would-be leader of Khazaria in Diaspora never knew Baghatur had saved his life.

Bihar watched the woman clutch her enormous belly.

White flashes probably whammed across her eyes, dizzily turning her into a hot pool of gore.

The blood across her black djellaba curled like spirals in a Khwarizm carpet.

A full--lipped woman, with the slanting-back forehead of an ancient Assyrian queen, the lady Parsbit, wife of Baghdad merchant Abdul Azziz fell nobly as a Caesar, turning the street again into a place where the air reeked of manure. From her body came a long, loud burr... of stinking bowel gas, like rotten eggs. Her mouth went crooked, dropping open loosely with a little broken groan.

Bloody vomit gushed from her lips down the side of her cheek into her collar. Her honey-colored oval eyes rolled up, so that only the whites showed, red-veined and dirty.

No one informed the future ruler of new Khazaria. The woman's whole frame sank from her own sight along with surrounding objects, leaving the pain standing forth as distinctly as a mountain peak, as if it were a separate bodily member. At last her agony also vanished.

The secretly chosen leader went on his way. The people applauded him. He didn't see what happened. The woman's kohl-lined eyes, long-lashed, the hennaed cherry-black braids became another winged griffin, and then shrunk to a butterfly Sphinx on an alabaster jar. Her tongue dropped to the side. From a distance she curled like a royal cat. The knees that-were bent up when she fell, now flapped open wide apart. Her baby's bottle had broken and spilled juice in a winding stream to the gutter. Her older son had slept in his litter through the lightening grooves that marked his mother.

The call went up for a healer, and Bihar came running, no longer dressed like the Kagan, the Khan of the Khazari. No one recognized him there, in Kiev, or in Atil anymore. Those who knew him already dispersed to the steppes. A woman leapt from the crowd to lift her djellaba. And bared her, exposing enormously fat thighs flapped apart, "haram," forbidden for anyone to see in public.

Her exposed belly, perfumed by orange blossom gums and frankincense, seen through spun silk fabrics showed the world that her husband had purchased cloth for her from a merchant along the Silk Road.

Her heaped-wheat belly rising like the dome of the Rock, was now ready to give birth. Before she started to decay, Bihar was directed by someone who resembled an outdated ancient Roman legion's general lost in the tenth century-- to rip open her belly with his obsidian blade and deliver the twin boys, healthy and bouncing within a few minutes.

The arrow had passed through her navel, between the two babies without touching them. She lay there, waiting for the maggots to swim through her brain. Her firm, large breasts filled with milk, lay partly bared by hands rushing to examine her in bewilderment.

Each nipple slowly sank from a brown bud into a calm, shriveled flatness, like two deflated balloons. All that prolific, Euphrates motherhood had whizzed out of the cow-goddess while the bow yards above unknowingly rocked and whined in the dusty wind, plucked by the Tarkhan like a one-stringed violin.

The lady became an artist at this moment. She captured the new leader's audience. A crowd of painted dolls with babies, and moustache-wracked men, mouths filled with pistachio nuts and "palace bread" candy came running from the merchant's stands, along the silk road, yards of cloth over arms.

Bihar didn't see the canvas that caught the artist's painting, Baghatur's portrait. He began to shed his few belongings and leave the rest, his rings, and his identity as a Kagan, with Baghatur.

He would have to find a way to get through the lines to a new homeland, but where? He thought. He only took a cloth sack.

"You can get away with anything because you are more a healer than a Kagan," Baghatur told him. "You can't go to Kiev. They will find you there. Where will you go, to Byzantium? They will find you there, too, and also in Armenia. Persia is not the right place. Do we go east or west, my Kagan?"

"I'll send for the Khatun and my son in the one place they won't find me. Let everyone else think I went where I can be the healer at the Caliph's court in Egypt or Cordoba."

When he finally left the area, Bihar felt so well again. He had donned the swaddling robes of an Imam. "No one stops a religious teacher on his most holy pilgrimage to Mecca. Look at my face.

Is this not the face of a pilgrim from Samarkand or a Pharaoh of the Nile?" Bihar was a nomad again riding against the hot wind of the road. "Cordoba is a lifetime away," he told his new traveling companions.

"Who will dare forget Jerusalem?" Bihar's eyes shone as he spoke in a quiet voice.

"You have no blood ties to the Jews of King David's Jerusalem."

"Neither did Ruth, the Moabitess."

"Ruth was a woman of the Syrian deserts."

"My Meotis deserts share the same sunshine."

"Why are we going to Jerusalem?" One companion asked as he rode beside Bihar.

"Cordoba is our new Jerusalem."

"All in good time. To get to Jerusalem, I must first create the right seals and parchments to become the healer to the royal court of the Caliph. Before I can do that, I must learn more about who really rules Jerusalem from behind the latticed shutters. I must enter Jerusalem only when I've first met my destiny in Egypt."

"I'm taking my family north by west," Baghatur said. "I need land to farm."

"And I seek people to heal," said Bihar.

"Perhaps I can make miracles happen again."

Walking to Jerusalem

On his way throngs of people under the olive trees were sleeping in the open air. They came from all directions "What's happening here?" Bihar asked. I did little more than follow my father's tracks, keeping up with him took great effort.

"We're not allowed to go back to the town," a priest told him. "They're burning the town."

"Who?"

"The children."

Two Khazari rabbis walked down the road carrying prayer books. One of them put a finger on his Cherkessk kindjal, a fine blade, as Bihar smiled and asked him," Is it heavy?"

They stood face to face. The other Khazar asked him where he was going.

"The new Jerusalem, Bihar replied."

"Don't go to Cordoba," the old man answered.

"There are too many Jewish healers and rabbis there already, and the Caliph is sending them to Egypt."

"Go directly to Jerusalem," the younger added, putting down his heavy sacks.

"I'm a healer, a man of a thousand disguises," Bihar sighed. "I speak many tongues, and I have torah scrolls to deliver that I sent on ahead also in disguise as alchemy formulas for healing."

"That's not a disguise. You can say the Torah can be used as a form of healing—of the soul and of the morals," another old man exclaimed with fervor.

"In Jerusalem you'll end up as a soldier in the army of Islam, if you disguise yourself as a pilgrim from Persia."

"I'm not going to go as a pilgrim from Persia. The Arabs will not know what to expect from a man of the Gobi deserts, perhaps from Samarkand or further east. Look at my fine cheekbones and the way my eyes slant down at the corners.

The herbs and Torah scrolls or these fine needles from Cathay with which I heal come from the great Silk road that runs from Cathay to Rome. And look at these healing needles so fine, the light passes through them. With these, I can heal my way across the world."

"The medicines are used up everywhere. Go north. You will be needed in the northern countries."

"Go to Karelia," the younger man interjected.

"No one will know you there, or care. You will be needed more than anywhere else." The two men turned around and left.

"No, I must go to Jerusalem and deliver these Torah scrolls from Kiev."

Nablus

The Khazarian Kagan's fine acupuncture needles from along the Silk Road's gateway to Cathay earned him the reputation of a miracle healer. Father and I found ourselves far from the caravans of his Silk Road, in Nazareth, amidst Christian Arabs who welcomed his skills as a healer and me as his helper.

Again, we were in disguise as there is no peace from those who come to our land from everywhere in the world looking to fill their needs, or for the answers to their problems in relics and talismans. People come here to find results, and it is a place of last resort. We came in peace. We found many people and many wars.

Father and his life-long friend, Baghatur, tarkhan of the Khazari, sat on this rooftop, drinking lemon tea from tiny cups and playing backgammon. It was easy to absorb the culture around us, but finding a kosher chicken in Nablus?

For that, the rabbis in Jerusalem, as few as they were, had pointed to those who came from the Black Sea ports and from Italia. Their kosher chickens freely scratched in the sand long before we arrived. Father and I are well here in Nablus as healers to all who walk these crossroads.

"The Christian Arab dwellers of Nazareth were relieved to see us," said the Bihar, the traveler. Baghatur long ago had joined Bihar in the Caucasus and went with him to the Holy Land to seek a new trade and a serene life.

"This is no land for warriors," Baghatur insisted. "All I want in my elder years is peace."

"The soldiers of Islam have always won." Bihar reminded him. "Maybe we didn't want to fight any more for what's outside ourselves when the courage we must fight for most lies inside us."

"I would have fought for a free Kavkaz, for the twelve tribes of the Cherkessk," Baghatur said.

"And what of the twelve tribes of Israel? Now that I've delivered the Torah scrolls, what is my reward?"

"The open crossroads you see here. Where else can you freely walk to Jerusalem holding your head up high as the Kagan of the Khazari? Not these days in Kiev."

"Are we really Levites, descendants of the lost tribe of Simeon?" Baghatur asked. "Or did our rabbis invent that story so we could all become priests in the synagogues of the world?"

"Why is it important to you? We Khazari have our own Levites and Cohanim. Once you become a Jew, you are commanded to forget what you worshipped before. All memory of the past before you took your oath is supposed to be erased. Yet you still wear that Turkic tamga around your neck, that pendant of your horse. Are you still sending

white horses to Tengri?

"What difference would it make? If you go back to a world before Abraham, we are all in the same boat together. Can't you see we come from and go back to the same place? The whole world is in that same boat together this moment--and forever."

"We'd be judged as traitors if we think that," Baghatur said as he scratched a twig along the earth-top roof. What's the difference between worshipping a golden calf or this horse pendant around my neck? Do you really think I worship it?"

"Is it the extra protection you need for good luck? Is that why you still wear it? What's wrong with wearing a menorah or putting a mezuzah on your door post? Why are you still wearing that last bastion of Turkic freedom to roam the steppe or the mountains of the Meotis?"

"It's just a good-luck charm."

"You don't need charms. Make your own luck. Take responsibility to lead yourself. You don't need a leader. Have you read your Torah portion? Think for yourself.

Remember action does more than faith."

"But faith heals the body when all other hope has failed and action no longer works."

"Why? Is Khazaria only a memory like faith when we need action? Isn't Khazaria a state of mind today?" Bihar looked at Baghatur sharply.

"Your own son doesn't even remember Atil. His children will never hear of it."

I had been listening from the bottom of the stairs. Now I joined the two older men on the rooftop garden.

"How would the Moslems here treat you if someday the other side—maybe Jews,

maybe Christians, maybe outlanders—win this land in battle?" Bihar asked. "It has been won before by many, and all have had their turn. What place will last forever?"

"Well, Islam won, and we Khazari Jews will be left as always during these wars," I told my father.

"See all these Christians here, and Moslems over there?" Bihar smiled.

"So?" I stretched his neck to hear my father's answer.

"Some of them are the descendants of Jews who lived here in the time of King David. And when the land changed owners, they took the religion of whoever held the power. Not all of them left. Only those who kept their beliefs or wanted land or a different life left. Many were forced to leave, of course, but not all."

Bihar shrugged and ate bread with me, for I was now grown at this time in the future. You see, I've traveled back in time again to tell you this tale while I'm age thirteen, but then, in that future, I was grown.

And so as my father's grown son, dipping my heel of bread in crushed garlic and olive oil, I told my father, "This land was not emptied when the Romans left.

There were those who stayed here because they wanted to, and other Jews from Damascus or Antioch came to live here as well as Christians and later Moslems. You see? We come from everywhere here. So why not from Khazaria, too?

"Do you really think because we left Khazaria that Khazaria left us? Who lives in Khazaria today? The same people who always lived there? Other people who came in later? And who lives next to those who were in Khazaria—the Iranic peoples--long before we Turkic tribes came, or all the people of Kiev?

"Who knows from where we began to roll our wagons? Who knows who we were and what language we spoke before our language was given to us by those whose tribes we joined? Maybe the steppes or maybe the deserts, or maybe the highest peaks of the mountains. That's the way it is everywhere when lands change hands."

I watched Baghatur sip his lemon tea. Bihar drank from his water skins as they made a fleshy sound slapping against the ruined stones.

"It's a small place to hide so many people who want to live near the sacred places. Too bad the places that have few people don't have more of these holy places that attract worship and trade.

For where there's worship, there's more trade," Baghatur added.

The next morning was another hot day in July, and Bihar went along the road between the fields of wheat. Women were starting to work the fields again.

The children carried sheaves on their heads. Everything had to be done by hand.

In Nablus, life went with no work. The food was gone and not enough healers yet. So Bihar was welcome to mix his herbs and alchemy because they made miracles.

He passed an old farmer wearing a large Greek cross. "Keev Halik?" In Arabic Bihar asked the man how he was.

"Forget me," the farmer waved back.

"Your crops are still rotting?" Bihar asked as he walked toward Jerusalem.

"I had to sell my farm cheap." The farmer laughed tensely.

"So did my forefathers in Sarkel," Bihar answered, with a pointed finger.

"Are you a Cherkessk Mountaineer?"

"What difference would it make to you from where I come? Does the left side of the Sea mean more to you than the right side of it? There's enough fish at both ends to feed the world."

"Where are you going?" The farmer shielded his eyes from the sun with his hands.

"I'm going to Jerusalem."

"Jerusalem? You see the thefts? That's the road to Jerusalem. So much is passing through the villages." The farmer spat. "Watch your gold."

"Highway robbers?"

"Many," the farmer nodded.

On the road to Jerusalem Bihar passed returned inhabitants and flattened mud brick houses. Children were sleeping in the rubble.

"No water." Bihar told the farmer.

Many had come back to the ancient village, returning to a wreck.

"There's nothing to eat. Go to Nablus," the farmer told Bihar.

When he arrived, Bihar found the children pounding on doors to beg food.

Older people were beginning to move back to the ruins. The inhabitants were refugees of another war, and Marót helped them rebuild small houses, now demolished again.

Bihar stood in front of the homes of the village elders. "I need bread--three loaves per family," he demanded.

"Go home, Mountaineer. Life has returned to normal," the elders told him.

"I'm not Mountaineer," he said in Arabic to the Christians. "Why is it so important to you to know what I am if I come as your healer?" I motioned to him to be silent.

"Go, Armenian," someone shouted to him.

"Find us bread to feed the children."

"Sure. Food must be more important to you than what I am. I am what I am--to myself and my family. It's not necessary that you know so you can label me, tax me, or conscript me into your army. It's not required that you track me whenever I enter or leave your lands."

"Yes, it is, for order, or else we will have chaos," a young man hastily replied.

The road again came into view, past Ramallah. Bihar saw three villages go to the bread kneaders. The houses were burned or flattened, but this time, he didn't know by whose soldiers.

"What side am I on now?" I asked my father.

"The side that God chooses you to be," Bihar said sadly.

"What if the divine will is that decisions are mine to make?"

"Father, we should have gone to Djerba. On that island, Jews live in peace."

"We are not welcome in Djerba because they believe Levites have been cursed."

"But we are Levites because we ourselves decided that we are Levites." I walked beside my father. "Can't we decide as well that we are Cohens and go to Djerba?"

Alone in the dead silence, donkeys scratched the ruins. Furniture was abandoned in the middle of the road. Pots were strewn about. There was no time to take anything. We stopped by an adjoining farm to watch the women and children cultivate fields that stretched beyond borders that changed each day.

Bethlehem

My father roamed the streets to watch the feverish selling. Who could succeed in selling a plate, a scarf, a trinket? Buyers bargained for the lowest price.

Each year a new army with a different belief tried to conquer the sacred land, in the way of too many cross roads of time and trade, its nation's coins became worthless. Bihar threw away his.

Boys dressed in white robes ran from one street vendor to the next. When the merchandise and foods on the Christian side were empty, the boys had to buy in the many more Moslem shops at three times the price.

The few Jewish bazaars remained hidden in houses behind shutters, houses along dark and winding streets that one could not find without knowing whom to visit. And there were still fewer stalls that served the Armenians, the Greeks, the Mountain Men, and European traders.

Every nationality had its niche from whom it bought food and trinkets. I asked my father what he thought as we looked at the array of diversity. Would he drink their coffee? Would he eat their food? Did they mix meat and milk at the same meal? Would he betray his many disguises? He healed all of them. "I am the miracle worker here," he told me.

I laughed back at my father. "All this change only means nothing will ever change on the inside."

Hebron:

Bihar, in still another disguise and different robes came to a tiny village and counted twelve flattened houses. "I wonder who is settling the accounts this time."

Soldiers of the Great Caliph rode near him. "Leave your houses if you want to save your lives."

"Peace be with you. *Salamoo aleikum.* I am El Hajj, on a pilgrimage to Mecca from Samarkand."

Bihar argued in a sing-song voice of Central Asia. He squinted and smiled widely, turning upwards the corners of his dark eyes, this time disguised in white robes as an Imam. I stood behind his robes bedecked in the garb of an Imam's apprentice holding his holy scrolls, water skins, and healing bag.

Father made sure he carried the correct scrolls to show to the soldiers—Arabic or Kurdish, or scrolls in the Turkic languages or the Persian with alphabets the toughest soldiers could read in Arabic. They had to let this holy man pass on his way to fulfill his pilgrimage. "When in the desert, do as the Bedouin," became our rule.

It was easier to pass as Silk Road pilgrims from the belly of Asia than to try to pass as Bedouins. The Arabic scrolls got us by. No one could read the Turkic alphabets unless they used the Arabic characters.

Even Khazar language scrolls would be unrecognizable in the Hebrew alphabet as a language. We took only the Arabic holy books and easily traveled from place to place without being stopped for long.

The last soldiers he met learned he was an Imam from Bokhara. He knew more merchant's watering holes along the Silk Road, their names, customs and dialects than the Emperor of Cathay.

Four Arab-speaking soldiers turned their horses. "Then be on your way, quickly."

He walked through the village looking for fresh horses of his own, but no one was around except the old people pouring out of the crumbling village.

An old Jewish woman tried to get Bihar's attention. "I think we're both in the wrong place today." He found himself wandering aimlessly.

The woman asked Bihar whether he was a Jew. Bihar nodded.

"A man didn't leave quickly enough because his wife went into labor. He was killed."

"You would have seen worse in Atil."

The woman touched the back of her hand to her chin. "And where I came from, if they thought you walked by their wells....It was even worse than that, and I'm far from your homeland."

"And where do I belong?"

Glances of hatred from below and above-- glances of contempt bore through his essence. Bihar passed through the crowds, his contorted face glistening. Leaves swept past him to the river as rootless as himself, and ropes of smoke curled around his white and gold robes.

A woman carrying a calabash on her head closed one eye and cursed, "May the earth move so their houses fall on their heads."

"Once you leave, you can't go back," a soldier shouted to Bihar.

He took the road to Jerusalem. "I'm an Imam on a pilgrimage to Mecca," he told the soldier. "I have permission to go everywhere."

He gestured back. "Peace be upon you."

"Be careful, I said. "Messages between separated families are forbidden."

"How many days to Jerusalem?" The soldier held up his hand.

Again, Bihar changed his disguise to that of a healer. Doors opened. It was dawn when Bihar awoke in Jerusalem. The sounds were maddening.

He eagerly sat by the gate. Bihar waited for fighting soldiers in the streets to pass by.

"Where did you learn Arabic?" A soldier asked Bihar.

"Baghdad. The Silk Road winds through many lands, all of whom need those who heal the lame."

He held up a bag of herbs, a sack of za'atr, the black seeds from Egypt that heal, and his fine acupuncture needles given to him by a merchant of the Emperor of Cathay when he was a young prince of the Khazari.

The needles had healed for thousands of years at the eastern end of the Silk Road. They had bought him his life and fortune wherever he traveled.

We went on. A priest arrived with three dying children on a bier. Father carried them into a sanctuary of shadowed arches, a place where in the lands he had seen, a Khan would have hidden wives behind silent, dark lattices.

He heard the sound of cool fountains on fragrant jasmine petals. All at once my father's freedom of action in a moment had become meaningless. A little trail of saliva left his lips.

"Why am I afraid to tell anyone who I am? No place is safer than the desert. It's only in cities that there is danger."

I grabbed my father's forearm. "When I grow up and marry what should I tell my children about Khazaria?"

"The truth." he said sharply. "And don't forget you also have family in Alania. You are as diverse as the Caucasus. Out of many people, one united spirit of resilience, one voice of confidence, one goal of love of all peoples and acts of kindess and healing. Repair and heal the world and bring much joy."

"And if I forget thee, O' Khazaria, will my left hand forget its healing?" I teased. "My right hand already is promised to Jerusalem for writing and praying."

"My respect for Khazaria is growing as deep as the calluses grow on my hands." My father went inside to guard the healing room's window.

"Use those acupuncture needles from the Silk Road to heal all and bring wisdom to those who ask to be healed. Educate and give charity."

Bihar complained how his throat clicked in tight knots. He rubbed his bag of herbs against his cheek, to make the fear go away. Bihar's eyelids fluttered and he dropped back, away from the latticed shutters. He gazed at the empty street. The walls around him seemed to evaporate. Terrible, silent tears dropped to his shoulder.

Exiled kings were not welcomed anywhere, he thought, but in Jerusalem, there was always an open door for a healer whose potions worked well with the poor and the rich.

Bihar covered his mouth with his forearm, as if to hide his own

darkness. Memories of a youth riding white stallions alongside grey wolves in Atil or Sarkel returned to both of us, and we spoke of them to each other. He remembered the years he had spent with his wife, the Khatun, a Jew from

Mashad, Persia, from the days he sailed from one end of the Sea of Meotis to the other that he recounted to me many times.

Jerusalem

I nudged him from his dream. "So this is Jerusalem," he said, nodding as he looked around.

"It should have felt different," my father sighed. "I feel a sense of exclusion in an off-limits city."

"What do you say we don our Islamic robes?" I asked.

"Yes," he answered twisting a fresh Imam's turban around his head. "Infidels are often assaulted in the bazaars. They are refused lodging in pilgrim's hostels and haircuts by barbers. We can dress this way, until the Christians come here. I keep the garb of a Bishop from Rome and the hooded head covering of an Armenian, a Byzantine priest's frock and a monk from— where is that place? Ah yes, Assisi.

"We have the dress of a wizir and the abaya, and here--put on these robes of a pilgrim on his voyage to Mecca. You never know who will win the next battle, so I always keep several sets of clothing—one for each faith.

"Father even dressed as a Mongol warrior. Look into my eyes. Can you really tell who I am?"

"Not really," father laughed. "We are a family without boundaries."

We could be a little of many peoples. "What about Jewish life here? Are there any others like us, from Khazaria?" I whispered.

"There must be some," Bihar replied. "It reminds me of the year I spent with your mother's family in Mashad. But that's Persia, not Khazaria."

Father often repeated how Jewish life in Mashad officially came to an end on the tenth of Muharram.

"Your mother reminded me that her family had no hope other than the grace of the Almighty, the coming of the Messiah, or the arrival of the Khazari."

"The arrival of the Khazari?" "Shalom," I laughed. "Since when would a Jewish woman of Persia marry a Khazar, and why not a Khazar of the lost tribe of Simeon?"

"When none beneath the Kagan could have this woman."

Father told me each time he remembered how he had been forced into the Caucasus. Jewish Hajjis had long been detouring through Mecca, leaving other pilgrims in Egypt so they swiftly could sail to Jaffa.

We found many secret Jews. In Jerusalem they prayed at both Moslem and Jewish holy places: the Dome of the Rock and the Western Wall. Bihar joined other secret Jewish hajji, one of a band of secret Mashadi Jews from Persia who came back to Persia from Mecca by way of Khazaria to bring other secret Jews the news of Jerusalem's growing Jewish settlement.

"My soul will not be flushed out into the bay through my grandfather's anger," father told me.

Now, aware of the wafting incense, the smells of Jerusalem, I focused my thoughts on the present. Music of the kanoun with its 86 strings wailed in nuances of delight in a distant room, and the spicy scent of cinnamon and kamoun crossed his senses. A bowl of fava beans was hurled from a window to join the garbage below.

"Men chip away at their old gods in their own images," father spoke as we walked cautiously in the holiest of holy cities. "Golden fingers hammer golden notes into symbols to be worn around the throat, so music can be frozen in time."

The old curse was unfeeling. The family was more important than each of its members. But in war without a family, you go crazy. This was my father's third war.

"It almost never rains in July." Father and I were startled by the feminine voice. At the same time, we whirled around to see the silhouette of two women standing behind us—my mother and Raziet-Serakh, my sister. Behind her stood her husband, Yusuf of Toledo, and her infant daughter.

"Mother! Raziet-Serakh!" I shouted. "Yusuf!" We hugged as father rushed to embrace all of us tightly. I heard him cry with joy at seeing the family together. He thought the Khatun would never have taken so dangerous a journey hoping to find us. We traveled. We never stayed long in any one place.

"The rain. It's pouring again. It never rains in July." Raziet-Serakh said softly, cradling her new daughter. "Meet your uncles," she laughed. She held up her child, and father took his first grandchild in his arms gently and kissed her on her chin.

Father cleared his throat. "Khatun, Raziet-Serakh….Yusuf--how did you get here without me?"

"I grew tired of waiting to grow, and I refused to grow old in the twenty years we could not find each other, my husband, the Khatun said softly. " I've heard from afar how you heal the sick, the tortured, and the old with those needles that old man from Cathay gave you and the time you spent learning from his students. Now you teach what others think is magic or miracles."

"In Kiev, you'd be burned as a sorcerer, Raziet-Serakh added. "Some fear the Silk Road's miracles. Others trade in miracles, and still others tax it. You forgot my Hebrew name. I'm now Shoshanna, the rose."

When Khatun spoke, everyone fell silent to listen. "I've learned much from you, as much as you learned from my peoples. So when word crept back that now you teach others to heal, I had to find my way. It was so hard leaving my daughter and her family. It's time I helped you finish what you came here to realize—to find your purpose."

Khatun leaned against the window sill. Father looked up at her sandstorm-weathered face. Her dark ash brown curls now were silvered. So were the birch trees of Khazaria he longed for but knew he would never see again unless my father time-traveled once more.

"I'll show you where I have been, where no one knows I'm the Queen of the Khazari, if you don't mind a place where the rain comes in."

"I have much to show you," Yusuf said. He led his horses, walking beside Khatun and Raziet-Serakh. "I had two choices—the resting place called Polin, or Jerusalem."

"How did they let you in this land?"

Mother answered, but everyone tried to speak at the same time. "My Arabic is as good as yours, but my Persian is better," mother continued.

No one interrupted her as she spoke. "For once having a wife from Mashad brought a blessing, a mitzvah to your life here. Who here can discern between the Queen of the Khazari and a village Arab of many seasons when both have that great equalizer, silvered hair?"

"Rain," Khatun sighed. "In Mashad it was forbidden for a Jew to go outside in the rain, for fear of contaminating rainwater which might then touch a non-Jew."

"I played many roles to get here," Bihar told her as mother embraced him. Mother and Raziet-Serakh hugged me, and I could be with my whole family again. Mother welcomed us home.

"I always wondered whether you really wanted a Persian wife from Mashad? Would you have preferred a Khazar? A woman of Baghdad whose father taught the Torah? All I know that it saved my life when I had to travel to Jerusalem. Like you, I became a woman of many disguises. I was a good Mountaineer Moslem from Dagestan whose family went to Persia.

"And being from Toledo I had no problem speaking my brand of Arabic," Yusuf said. "Living in Polin or in Kiev, though, you don't get too much practice in it, but the Khazar tongue abounds in Polin's villages as does Hebrew and the Frankish dialects."

"Like you, I did the same," my father added. "I played Imam from Tashkent on a pilgrimage. The Silk Road is an open book of many peoples. All you had to play was a mother of nations. Could this only happen in Khazaria, my queen?"

"Or in Mashad?" She looked at him like a dove.

Mother and I sat beside my father, the Kagan of the Khazari. Raziet-Serakh and her daughter sat beside me and Yusuf at my side, towering over me. It was an eternity ago that father talked so freely, that the family healer no longer had to disguise himself as a king without a country.

A Kagan should be a healer, whether in his country or any other. A healer must restore to wellness not only the sick of mind and body, but those who need to pray. The Kagan always was the spiritual leader of Khazaria.

The Bek ruled the government, and the Tarkhan commanded the soldiers. That's why Khazaria to us now in Jerusalem, is a state of mind. Where will we go to find peace? Inside ourselves.

"Jerusalem is the only city to which kings without their lands return," mother said.

"It's where everyone crosses paths with everyone else." I concluded.

"So where do we go from here?" Father looked wide-eyed at all of us.

"Listen." father interrupted.

"I don't hear anything."

"Neither do I hear a sound."

"That's it. The silence. Not even a bird is singing."

"The fighting has stopped."

"For how long?" Khatun asked. "Trouble is coming from the West."

"There always has been trouble in the East, and the North and South are engaged in fierce battles."

"Everyone here has a different language and a different faith."

"It was also like that where we came from and every place else that we went to."

"And that's how it always will be in all the crossroads of the world."

"No one will remember our language in Khazaria."

"Khazaria also was a crossroad of the world. So was the Silk Road."

"Where shall we go? Where shall we stay?"

"This is next year, and we already are in Jerusalem."

"So is everyone else who wants to come here."

"Where should we go?"

"All I need is a garden."

"For centuries, the empire of Khazaria reached from the Black Sea to the Sea of Meotis with many allies, and in one day, my whole pagan country turned Jewish…..and all of a sudden, we heed the laws of Sinai, and Khazaria is no more," I told mother.

"When Jerusalem turned Jewish, she, too had her temple destroyed by Rome," mother replied.

"Maybe we had it coming," Raziet-Serakh echoed.

"Nobody ever has anything 'coming,' my father said. "We make our own destiny through our choices."

"Maybe there's a jinx on this place…or on Khazaria. In the open steppes, no one came to us.

"We should look for the open spaces."

"There was famine in the steppes and open places after all those dry, hot winters and rainless summers," my father added. "We are in the crossroads of the world, here. Don't say what you'll regret, my son."

"We must find a place to go where there is peace, but where there is peace, there is no food or water," mother said. "Where shall we go?"

"We'll be given a sign pointing to our destiny," my father sighed. "In the time I have lived here, there was no peace. Each one of us makes peace within himself and then within his own family. That's the only way peace will come to the world."

"Only when there is enough food, and less taxes will peace come," I said.

Khatun, Raziet-Serakh, Father, Yusuf, and even my sister's new baby listened to the energy in one another. Metal became flesh and human turned machine.

"You were right that the more things change, the more they....." Khatun was interrupted by a rabbi walking down the cobbled stones with a crooked stick.

"They say you can heal...Please come. I need you to help my children." Bihar and Khatun brought me with them. I followed in my father's footsteps as a healer and learned the energy points of the needles and the herbs of all the lands we have covered. "Let me help and learn, too," Yusuf begged.

"The more help we have, the more we can do for all these people around us," father shouted, waving us over to join him as we scurried to make whole was broken.

"Yes, all of us will be with you. This is my son, Marót, and here is my husband, Bihar, and our family, but here you may call him Nissim."

"Nissim?" The rabbi said with a wide smile as he nodded to a Greek Father passing beside him, and then to the local Imam. "It means miracles."

The years go forward, and still we remember our magnificent Alania and all the peoples of all the lands we have experienced with great joy. For all the lands we have lived in for generations are written in our containers for us to remember with much love.

#

--- ⚰ ---

Sister, now it's your turn to continue the tales of exquisite Khazaria and of magnificent Alania and of the great joy of the wonderful dances of Karachay and Balkaria. Remember all of them with good tidings.

Dear Diary:

I'm back. It's me, now known as the rose of Yerushalmi. I will soon decide which Hebrew name I will take. And for now, I am trying out several names. And yes, I've remembered to write down my name from Alania, and from Karachay, and from the Balkarians, and the name given to me by the Kagan and Khatun of the Khazari.

So many years did we live in Jerusalem, until one day, the family went into the mountains and found a hole cut in the rock that seemed to lead us deep into the earth. So many names...

At least a thousand lives time traveled in the span of so many years and so many more to experience with the joy of life. The time capsules, living legacies, and memorabilia with the literature still records in words, dance, and song our experiences.

The entrance looked exactly like the exit of the cave we found in the Kafkas, near the land of the Avars. And wouldn't you know it? Again, we were driven into that cave in the rock by a great golden whirlwind that drew us in.

And when we awoke again at the other end of this band of time, we were not in Jerusalem, but back in the first cave, after all, as if all this were a dream. Let me tell you how I time-traveled back to age sixteen once more, even after my own children were grown and we had settled as healers in Jerusalem.

Where do you go on a vacation when you already live in the promised land of milk and honey? You know how many promised lands in which we have lived? I'm looking beyond for promised worlds in my time traveling adventures. Worlds so green, so uninhabited, way out there in space just waiting...for projection, imagination, and travel.

My next adventure, perhaps...In our minds, we can create a story from *nothing* and travel back and forth in time and space. If I can create a story from *nothing*, (*nothing but the chemistry and electricity of thought you can measure in the brain with computers as I travel to your time zone*) then life can be created from dark energy in space, a kind of force that repels gravity and keeps the galaxies from moving apart too quickly. Ah, but I'm digressing from my beloved Alania.

You go back to the golden age of where you're from when you had a kingdom of your own— back to our orchards in Atil and Sarkel when it was in its bloom in the year eight hundred sixty of our Common Era, but first we took a little detour into the metallic future.

It seems as if I've been everywhere else, Dear Diary. You see, I could never be a princess in Jerusalem in the same way I was a princess in Khazaria. And power doesn't corrupt, it only teaches you to appreciate and collect art. See, that's why I travel in time back to my beloved, magnificent Alania when I want to savor that travel experience as therapy with the music of healing.

Once you have art, you have music. And when you have music, you have perfect mathematics, and then from those geometric forces, you have science. When you have science, you have letters. And music becomes a tool of healing.

That's why I had to diversify. How else could I find a nice vacation homestead once more in the golden age of Sarkel? Living in a crossroads of the world is one choice, but for a vacation in the heat of summer, the Volga can't all be contained in the sound of my golden musical instruments. Joy and laughter is good. A light in a dark room is good when you want to wake up. To find it, I listen to the musical sounds of the world as a healing tool. Imagination can make a story out of well, a daydream.

***

CHAPTER FOUR

———————— ⚔ ————————

The Middle of World War Two,
the Caucasus Mountains

S uddenly the family and Taklamakhan were in the Kafkas among the Mountaineer tribes, and not only a hundred years thrown into the well of the future, but now closer to a thousand. Here's how we found out where we were.

We awoke somewhere in the Kafkas. A piece of parchment or something with big black inky letters flew by, and I caught it. The numbers were strange.

They looked like this—1942. Is that where we were now? The big machines that moved had Teutonic lettering, like the Frankish knights or the men of the upper Danube who had often traded with Khazari on the Volga.

Our traveling rabbi friend from Spire recognized the dialect spoken by these men and their metal elephant-like armor is a form of the Germanic language. This he understood, albeit strange and different. Yet he was able to tell a little what they were saying. Going in advance of arms, the Germanic speakers penetrated into the fastness of the mountaineers.

My father whispered, "These foreigners are going to take advantage of the mutual jealousy of the tribes--Mountain Men against Tatars.

Taklamakhan motioned to us. "Look at those flags in the villages. They are all sons of Allah now. This region belongs to Islam. A Tatar has to be wise, or else how would we have conquered Rome with all her book learning?

"Put away those shields with the wandering stars of Atil on them. Don't advertise that you have just turned Jewish. They probably are looking for fellow sons of Allah."

We hid, but tracked them going from village next to village, fanning the hate of private feuds, widening the breach between the two hostile religious sects of Islam, we learned from the speakers of the Adyge language among us. The language hadn't changed that much in this hidden place so high in the mountains.

We heard what sounded like the language of the Rus coming in from the front, chasing the speakers of the Germanic dialects from the mountains of the Kafkas, and the Moslem tribes were marching against them. We hid in the empty, burned out huts of the Mountaineer tribes.

"Von Liebnitz," someone shouted the name of one of the Germanic commanders whom we learned was from Bavaria. Our mountaineer friends translated, as we heard their language had not changed enough to lose all understanding in this new time into which we were hurled.

"Send this request to Arslan, khan of the Kasi-Kamucks, in whose territory was Jarash that he should seize upon the person of the mollah."

Then the Mountain Men translated that "Arslan, afraid to lay his hands upon a teacher so holy to the people, took the mollah to the adjacent city of Avaria."

So that's where we were, near Avaria. The word went out across the birch trees and into all the small wooden homes: "Believers forget your sectarian differences. Members of different tribes, mountain men of every warring tribe, Tatars, join together and lay aside your animosities. All lovers of your country rise in arms and drive back the dogs who had dared invade the sanctity of the mountains."

The Bavarian frothed at the mouth, glad the crowd under took the Cherkessk dialect. Atokay walked right in like he had been living here in these times. "No mountaineer shall ever be a slave!" The word went out. But how many of their women had been sold into slavery by the warring tribes on different sides? But they were a new faith now.

"The first law of our prophet is the law of freedom. No Moslem shall be a slave." The word went out. Hmm. Something to ponder. But we, Khazari are now Jewish. The Mountain Men are not, yet they are people of the book. The cheers rose all night. Now, where do we stand? I don't see the difference between peoples.

Our Mountaineer friends led us into the homes of other Mountain Men, and we Judaic Khazari blended in with the rest of the mountain people of the Kafkas. They hid us well and didn't ask where we came from, only warned us that there was a war.

Our Turkic dialects, they didn't understand, but the North Kafkas speech of Atokay was still barely distinguishable, and they might have thought we had come out of Central Asia or somewhere by the Sea of Meotis far away and had joined to help them.

For the moment we kept our mouths shut and let them care for us until we could find our way back to the cave and get back to the glory of our own times and the orchards of our own Khazaria. The Ciracassians had a leader they called Murat. He came home from his long ride to Jarash and greeted us as fellow mountaineers, obviously in hiding from the men in the big metal elephants.

Our clothes had not changed much, with the exception of the chain maile and helmets that were stared down and laughed at until we removed them—or at least the men. "Actors," Atokay smiled in his dialect. "Theatre of the mountain men," he nodded.

The silence became unnatural. It was a silence that swallowed all sound and smothered it, a silence vibrating like a drum skin. Atokay stared at his bare feet and slowly moved the toes. They looked uncanny, as though his feet led a life of their own. He felt the fur of his blanket and the pressure of a servant girl's hand under his neck.

"You're a mountain man, and we are all going to be liquidated," Murat warned Atokay and our Kagan, who still pretended to be a man from the Caucasus.

Where was the "physical liquidation" to take place? Murat pointed out of the window to a Germanic commander a few feet away. Look what we walked into in another time. Murat called them Germans and reminded us that in 1942 the Germans were here in the Caucasus, and we would be liquidated.

"Why?"

"Ask him," Murat laughed. "Smell the leather of Von Liebnitz's revolver belt and listen to the crackling of his uniform."

"What's a revolver?" All of us asked at the same time. Father smelled the pork stink on the breath of the German soldiers. What did will he say to his victims?

We decided to be survivors. "The Russians are coming." Murat added.

"Rus? Is that who you mean?"

How would the Russians look? Would they call us ancient Khazar enemies when they came?

Murat, Atokay, and the Kagan all looked at their fingers. It was so quiet that we heard the crackling of the burning embers in the small fire pit.

"Do you feel ill, Murat?" His wife, Tanya's quivering whispers broke the silence with a shock.

All Murat's muscles contracted at once. Fear was beginning to seep into the hero. He blinked at her.

"Please, some water?" Tanya sat up and extended her hand praying to receive a tender touch. But he just stared blankly out of the window watching the war pass by. War drew his soul into the mountain.

I watched my father, the Kagan in hiding as Murat, the Mountaineer made his speech in front of the gathering tribes. Then I wandered about the small cabin waiting for dawn, waiting until those around me woke for prayers.

Someone motioned to Togrul, the little Pecheneg boy in my care. He helped the older men take down the red-gold and green-blue prayer rugs and brushed them clean, laying them down facing east. The women had washed and stood still, listening to the silence between the white-washed walls.

The rain had stopped as suddenly as it began, and the new silence hit all of us as a new color. The dawn had now come to meet me from the deep well of sanity.

Gradually the people of Himri had to take refuge behind the village's triple walls. During the retreat, the warriors who had been compelled to fight with the Germans gradually fell off, one by one Murat told Atokay.

Their chieftain's deserted them as they saw the superiority of the forces of the enemy. Even the principal Murid, Hamid Bey we were told was deceived, by forged proclamations issued in the name of the prophet separated himself from a leader whose fortunes were on the wane.

And when October's fallen leaves were still covering the hills of Himri, the Rus bayonets arrived to add their gleam to the tired mood of autumn, brown leaves choking a stream. We marked the cave in the Kafkas. How, oh, how were we going to go back through that opening in the dark rock?

How are we to go back to our own times? Back to a time when Khazaria was at peace and was in the midst of that excitement and joy of just having turned Jewish, and dancing and song were everywhere?

"The Mountaineer dream will be rolling up aoul Himri behind the roll of drums," Tanya whispered before she began to pray.

"One bullet will be mightier than a million forced votes when freedom is gunned down," said Murat.

"What's a bullet?" I asked. Is it like a pullet? The crowd of men showed us how time had changed, but everything remained the same.

"Would you rather be paid in a handful of flour or in knowledge?" Murat asked

Atokay, who translated for my father.

"Our mountains are being used as a shield," Murat said sharply.

The story passed along to me was that The Rus who are now called Russians are at war with the Mountain Men, the peoples of the Kafkas, but the Mountain Men only go to war with their own rulers.

So the thousand years or so that we'd been thrown into this future, not my future, nothing has changed the mighty mountains. Why did the people even come here eons ago from the Middle East?

"You have to rise above the law," Murat announced.

"No, you have to bring love and peace to all these people," my father said.

"How, by joining hands in death so others may live?

"No way," I insisted.

Tanya's large green eyes widened. She began to speak and Atokay translated the North Kafkas dialect that hadn't changed much in a thousand years.

The Rus were holding their chief men as hostages in Andrejewa. Atokay watched Murat smoke his chibbuk, a Mountaineer pipe.

"Bide your time," my father put his word in through the translator. "Are you so child-like as to believe that invaders from one land or time are any better than invaders from another?"

In Avaria was an Amazon-like woman who called herself a "Khatun" and re-named herself Pashu Bikay, a direct descendant of the she-khan who ruled in the winter of 1830. Pashu Bikay approached us and unveiled herself before the circle.

She cried out, "Go home you who came from Chunsash, and tie your rifles to your wives' corsets."

Amazingly, the men followed Pashu as their leader just as the Pashu who came before her. The crowd of men told me that eight thousand men followed this female, Pashu.

In the morning, a Germanic general, Von Liebnetz appeared, and I was told through the translator what this so-called second world war was all about. Oh, no, not in the midst of another war! I want to go home, back to the peace of Khazaria. The streets of Tarku were all torn up by war.

Gradually, each resident of Himri had to take refuge behind the villages' triple walls. So we were still in Himri, in the place of our summer home far from Atil, but thrown a thousand years into a future not our own and not by choice. I had to find out why. That's why the time-travels of the Silk Road continue.

Our hosts briefed us on what artillery was and the weapons of modern warfare, and I'd rather dance with the Bulgars than be here. And when the fallen leaves covered Himri, the Rus arrived to add their gleam to the mood of the end of summer.

Artillery soon brought down the towers of loose stones over the devoted heads. By that time, all of us found a common language, classical Arabic. We all spoke it, since the days when the great rabbis of Baghdad went forth into Khazaria with their Torah scrolls. When we wrote in Hebrew, we also had to translate from the Arabic for the scholars and rabbis from Toledo, so we learned many languages.

Pachu Bikay met the Queen of the Steppes, but Pachu still wanted to take up arms against the Rus like the Khatun had a thousand years before.

"I was born laughing," Pachu said through the translator. I watched as her face marred by the pox caught the rain in small pockets that glistened in the sun when the rain stopped. Our rainbow Kaganate also glistened. She lived by the art of war. We Khazari, vowed now to live by the art of Hebrew script, even if it meant losing our own language and culture.

I sensed a lack of unity among these tribes. We followed the men as they rode from aoul to aoul calling upon warriors to follow them. Each looked for a hero to lead him. The tribes of the Eastern and Western Kafkas seemed to be different. They sang the praises of heroes. My father told them to sing a little less and make more charts, but the chorus of voices sang louder and without ending.

Everyone still rode horses over a narrow, rugged path that winded over the mountains picking its way along the rocky bed of the torrent. Our horses dived into forests tangled with brambles. The horse of a Khazar or a Mountaineer is conscious that it is going to meet armed men.

***

Chapter Five

A Chorus of Voices

We came out of the past and met men living in our past, men on horseback with no big elephants, or tanks as they told us, in an age of tanks. Each warrior dressed like a Khazar as if time had not passed, wearing their shaggy bourkas that covered the entire rider and the back of his steed.

We had arrows, but they had what they said were "rifles." And the barrels of their rifles protruded from their long bourkas. Below dangled the horse-tails braided with bullets, just like the Khazar warriors who carried their arrow heads that way. So nothing really changes in the mountains or in the steppes like it would have if we were at the crossroads of the world. We are not. Those of the steppes soon take to the eagle's nests.

We stopped for the night. Murat seized his son and rode on a raid. He lived by the art of war. We lived by the book. I sensed these tribes needed a hero, but fast. What they had was the running fire of the guerilla as a power game.

Murat's son, Lam, rode from aoul to aoul calling upon warriors to follow them. We rode with them to a spot chosen to hold an assembly— in a vale shaded by trees.

Instead of making war charts, they sang praises of heroes. Murat determined his plans by a chorus of voices. A moonless sky paraded before us as we sprang into saddles of sheep's wool.

We were still in the Kafkas, but in the "year" as they call it, 1942, the party told us and explained in a way that they didn't know we weren't from their time. A narrow,

rugged path winded over the mountains picking its way along the rocky bed of the torrent.

Stopping to rest, the greenish tea passed before our noses. Murat cooked better than Taklamakan and prepared hot burghoul wheat and barley cakes with a savory pilaf of minced mutton. I poured honey over dried fruits.

The war would have to stop when it was time for cooking. Mountain men passed bowls of skhone, or mead with a little seasoned sour milk and a few honey and millet cakes. Everyone shared the food as they shared life.

Murat's son was silent, and so was my brother. They were both boys of the same age, that special ritual of transition that began in the future when a child turned thirteen and became responsible… when you dress as a warrior, but are still a little boy with a big job to save your family and your homeland while learning great wisdom.

The food eaten, every man took to cleaning his weapons while uttering a short prayer for protection. No speaking to one another. The sentinels were set. Each man knew that if he fell down in battle, he would only be a sleeping baby, the sky his crib's curtain.

I cut branches for them and covered the branches with mats and felts. It began to rain and a wind rose up. The boughs furnished us a place to nap. The men couldn't sleep well. They kept the watch fire burning out of the rain. Fires lighted up the whole mountainside making the granite glow with eerie colors.

Rocks snuggled against one another. The radiance warmed our faces. The enemy's fire, still the same old enemy, diffused a glow. Where were we now? The Kuban River still flowed as it had in my time. Whoever made the war, set fire to the reeds on the Kuban and Terek rivers meant to destroy the huts of the mountaineers.

Shadows threw a dull red tint on the horizon. Oh, my beloved Mount Elbrus, land of my earliest ancestors that I can remember from my childhood. There's the moon, a thin line of silver, rippling the blackness, outlining the sides of tanks hidden in a dark forest.

"Never take an enemy's life in cold blood," Murat whispered to my brother. He did not answer, but moved to kiss my father's hand, touching it to his forehead, and kissing it again before letting the Kagan's strong hand drop slowly to his side.

The Mountaineer's leader looked us over. "If you do not fear, there is nothing that can harm you. The horse's head will be turned toward the mountains."

Murat's son paced back and forth. "You tell me what tanks do?"

My father answered them all, a stranger in a strange land. "The Creator of all of us must help your enemies. We Khazari can do without outside help when it comes to fighting the enemy of our brothers in the mountains."

"Ah, but we have outside help," Murat grinned.

"Might they be the Russian hirelings? The free men of the mountain have spies along the border. Everywhere there are souls which can be bought for gold."

"War is not hell, son," Murat told his boy. "It's a poet's paradise."

"It is too, hell," the Kagan responded quickly.

"I'd rather be listening to the music of my water wheels."

"A poet fights better because he has read or written the romance of war," Murat said.

"Romance?" My father laughed.

"Yes," said the Mountaineer leader. "Our enemies, like the Roman legions cut off in the woods of Germany, will be left with no one to bury them. Each foreigner who comes in here to make war thinks more of his hut in his own land. Then one of us, unable to rest, rides down from the mountains and hides for a day in the reeds of the Kuban river."

Murat's son continued the vision, "We creep at night like a wolf from his lair. We glide unseen by the guard post of the enemy as the war-makers take their final pull on a vodka bottle. We crawl up within sight of him, and pick him off."

"And who is this enemy you speak of?" My father asked.

"Where have you been? Don't you know there's a World War on?"

"You are not thinking real," said the Kagan.

"You'll all perish. I haven't received any invitation to a war."

"You're in it now," Murat scowled.

We were all in this together, people from different times and different lands. Here and there small parties appeared in the distance. The method of warfare up here in the mountains hadn't changed since my times.

The men rolled stones on the heads of the enemy below same as they did twenty thousand years before. At Gogatel, a small fort situated south of the Andian range that runs parallel with the Andian branch of the Koissu, Murat and Atokay joined a tribe of mountain men.

Now, we all pitched in, Khazar from a distant time and Mountaineer mountain men from another time like two ends of one candle. We helped those around us to establish a depot of such provisions and munitions of war. This place, I'm told is a

single day's journey from Dargo.

The soldiers, lightly laden, set off at dawn full of cheer and energy. Before they tired, the men had crossed the pass of Retchel into the beech woods of Itchkeria. I am the only female in this pack of wolves. And then the fight begun.

Hostile tribes of the region were up in arms, and waiting for the enemy. The woods are deep here. As Murat's vanguard reached the first narrow ledge, a murderous fire from behind broke loose from behind the trunks of a thousand trees.

Lost in time. Lost in the woods. We scattered, not knowing what monstrous machines these men of the future had. Again, in the Kafkas, the more things changed, the more they didn't.

The mountain men fell across the path, serving as a shield for one party and obstacles to their enemy. They never explained who the enemy was, but they were fighting the Rus or what they later told us were the Russians on one side and the Germans on the other and also other enemies of the tribes of the Kafkas.

We had barricades—natural vines and flowercreepers. The paths were narrow and steep like in our summer palace away from the river flies. The winding path made the march so difficult that both us and whomever the enemy happened to be at the moment, none of us could march more than a few steps in a day.

Why were we fighting people we had never met? They told us about the war against the Jews and their war for a free Kafkas and the world war, and it all rang together like a giant gold bell.

Fighting went on into the night. Murat brought us close to Dargo. Flames and fire consumed this aoul, and the burning lighted up our path. Murat had set on fire every bit of wood, straw, and grain that could not be taken away. He left the enemy only the blackened stone walls of the mud houses.

"So you want to be a mountain man, eh?" I said to my brother, Marót. Our Mountaineer friends cooked their meals on the bivouac fires. We slept under the open sky. The next day more fighting came to us on wild horses.

Murat had found a force of six thousand warriors of the Kafkas to anonymously join up with this village called an aoul. The warriors opened fire on the Russians who were supposed to save the mountain men from Teutonic lands. We finally learned the name of those on each side.

An arrow wasn't good enough, or a stone. We had to learn the guns. And the guns consumed too much ammunition to be fired with any rapid movement. When the mountaineers took the weapons, they could not operate the Russian equipment they had taken. Someone took Dargo, but it wasn't Murat.

"In Medieval times," it has been said, 'when the Jews of Eastern Europe had no hope other than the grace of the Almighty, the coming of the Meshiach (Messiah), or the arrival of the Khazari,' we saved the battle for those we defended," said my father.

"We're time traveling again. This must be our purpose," I told all of them. We already know the future for Khazaria. Things don't get any better for us."

"It will," my father answered. "We have a purpose."

The Russians sent half of their force back to Gogatel to grab a supply of provisions. They had to push though the woods to regain their line by the north route. This move on Gogatel gave our brothers, the mountaineers another chance at their

enemies. But who was our enemies—those who were now called the Russians or the Germans?

"You're Jews. What do you think?" Murat assured us.

"And we're also Khazari," I answered. "And what do you think?"

"We certainly remember tales of the Khazari." Murat nodded. "But we learned of them through books written by the Russians."

The mountain men had given themselves no rest. Not satisfied with the slow work of the rifle, they now rushed in on the battalion tanks with only knives and expected to fight hand to hand. I still had to learn all about tanks and rifles, but with Murat at their head and strengthened by reinforcements, they attacked the escort party both going and returning.

With a war like this, who needs Khazaria's battle with the Kievan prince? Rain made the battle muddier. Along came a general named Klucke. He was a German deserter who still fought the Russians in vain. Now he asked to join the Mountain Men. When he arrived at Dargo, he had left thirteen hundred of his men, together with two captured Russian generals behind in the woods.

Three hundred mules with packs and wagons overflowing with grain stood next to cannons. And the mules and wagons fell into the hands of the Russians as all of us watched still hidden deep in the woods.

Soldiers were put on half rations (as they called their nomadic meals) and the horses ate the grass. Through the valley of the Aksai, a battle left scars on the earth. Murat's mountain men fought the battalions step by step s they retreated. Wherever the mountain of pain stood forth to the banks of the Aksai, only a narrow passage was left for their troops. Barricades blocked the way.

The mountain men took aim from behind the rocks and the beech trees as they brought down so many that the Russians took to their tanks. Murat sent for reinforcements so his men wouldn't fall into enemy hands. Fortunately for the mountain men, a band of Tatars carried messages to the fortress of Girsel.

The Tatars got through the barricades and brought the news of what was happening to the Mountain Men. Then three thousand infantry and three hundred Cossacks under a German named Freitag ran to their relief. The joy of the famished battalions could be painted in a portrait.

So nothing has really changed in this part of the world since the glory days of Khazaria, nothing except the shape of the metal and the reach of the weapons. We still didn't know who we were fighting and for what.

All we knew is that there is a war against the Jews and the German's wouldn't want us to survive. And when the Russians found out we were not only Jewish, but Khazari, they, too would be the enemy of us and the mountain people.

It was a time when everybody hated you because your people migrated to a certain place to find food. We asked now, just like we asked in Khazaria, where are we going to go to find a homeland?

Everyone thought the impenetrable mountains would stop the columns of soldiers. If it didn't stop the Khazari with arrows, why would it stop anyone else with elephant-like tanks?

What were we doing here, trying to liberate Kabarda? The fall of Dargo was a gray tedium that went through everyone, regardless of his tribe. These are the mountains. The Kabardas, great and small, lie on the northern side of the Kafkas range halfway between the two seas, northwest of the Lesghi and Chechen highlands.

If only there wasn't war. The green valleys, the broken, dappled mountains would undulate in the center like Khadife velvet on a Khazar's horse.

Army after army crawled out of the north, fresh from the tomb of men, and inexhaustible. Bulwarks circled the free homes of the highlanders. The Pagan days seemed to live on, even though the mountaineers are Moslem now.

Yet these mountains are Pagan as the ghosts that live in the rocks and the spirits that live in the trees. So we were in the Mountaineer militia now. A group of Khazari Jews and friendly souls from Alania in the middle of a Moslem militia back near Mount Elbrus and Mount Kazbek so far into the future for those that travel in time between ancient and medieval meadows.

We were drafted to be among the warriors, the hot young bloods who simply liked to fight. Every man wanted to through off his yoke. Independence was the word now as in our homeland and time. Finally, Murat had sent his zealous partisan, Ibrahim to lead an armed force that hoped to compel the Kabardians to take sides with him. Was there no other choice than war or to be a zealot?

Fearing the Russian tanks and the German tanks, the Kabardians preferred to stay neutral. No matter how much Murat asked them to riot against the Russians, they preferred to perfume their beards. Then the deportations started. Many of the mountain men were marched village by village to the deserts of Kazakhstan. Murat made a speech, "The enemy has conquered Cherkei and taken Akhulgo, and murdered the women of Avaria.

When lightning strikes one tree, does every other tree in the forest bow down to the storm and cast itself down should the lightning also strike them?"

My brother watched Murat closely. The speech went on in front of the Kabardins.

"You think for a moment they think of you as Russians? Is not your passports stamped 'Tatar' or stamped with your religion?"

"Don't you get the feeling we Khazari are undesirables here?" Mother whispered to me.

"I think those Moslem Kabardins feel the same way about the people who rule them. What do you say we get out of here?" I answered her.

Murat went on: "One branch rots and the whole tree goes to ruin. I shall protect you. Fight for your faith. Words won't work any longer. Now deeds will."

Everybody likes the idea of fighting for your faith, but there are so many types of faith, and just who is the enemy? No, this war thing won't due at all. I watched Murat walk away to his quarters.

On a pole a breeze trembled through a proclamation sign put up by the Russians. My Mountaineer friend translated and told me it read, "The commotions and bloodshed that have

taken place among the Caucasian Mountaineers have attracted the most
serious attention of Stalin."

Now who in the world is Stalin? Sounds like the name of a type of horse. Stalin the stallion. I had to find out. Troops already had arrived. I sensed a lot of people in this insane war had lost hope. In Khazaria we say when you lose hope you lose all fear.

What's good about that? I met a young lady my age that was from one of the Mountaineer tribes, the Adyge. She began to teach me her language and I followed her through these neutral fields of Kabardia. Her name also is Raziet. We had run out of time in this place, but unless we could get back to that dark cave and the secret opening that could hurl us back through time to the same place, we would never get back to Khazaria.

For in my time Khazaria was in its greatness, and I didn't have to worry about what would happen to it in a hundred years. Yet it seemed such a waste to only have lasted only so short a time. If there was only something I could do to change my homeland's fate. To take these people back in time with me and defeat the enemy would be wonderful. But that was not the time I was born into. Enemies couldn't make a dent in Khazaria in my time.

"Let's ride in the apple truck," Raziet motioned to me with hand signs and her words that I quickly learned. "In this year your destiny will be decided," she told me.

I decided everyone around me was no match for a war of this size. "My father has a plan for raising a troop for the crossing of the Kuban," Raziet explained.

"Sheik Mansour from the Eastern Kafkas will give my father three thousand men."

"I still don't know who you are fighting. Is it the whole world against the Kafkas? I thought this was the war against the Jews."

"And everyone else," she told me. I began to understand her language.

"Hey, Raziet, my friend. Are you talking three thousand men against the whole Russia? Or is it Germany you're fighting now?"

Nothing was clear to me anymore. Not only had I to deal with a time leap, but now sizing up who was fighting who and for what kind of freedom and independence. All I saw were messengers riding from one end of the mountains to the other.

And they were using the same horses we used, and it seemed everyone else was riding in those big tanks. I looked around. Peaceful highlands to my right and left. All I saw were the blossoms.

A steed cropped the first tender blades in the vale. A Lesghi sat listless at the door of his sakli basking without a thought of war. He watched the wooden beams of his home. The birds chirped, and I saw a turtle moving slowly in peace, half-asleep.

Then came the shouting. "Drag him down. He is the alien. He will kill us all by pulling us into a useless fight against an unseen enemy. Pull him down with ropes."

All of the men of Himri, Akhulgo, and Dargo, the riders of Arrakan and Gumbet, Avaria and Koissubui, Itchkeria, and Salatan, the people of the four branches of the Koissu, the bloodstained banks of the Aksai—all of them gathered here.

Lesghi, Chechens, warriors of Dagestan. Tribes of mixed Khazar and mountain origin, freemen all, speaking a basket of dialects sat in stirrups when they couldn't find jeeps. Guns and rifles rode at their side where Khazar arrows had gone before them.

Their leather bags were filled with cracked wheat. Few could afford what they showed me were called "cars." "Pull him down," the men shouted at Murat. No one had to pull him. He stepped down to meet the crowd who cheered.

Raziet and I, like stick figures, were pushed into the crowd. I found out the men here were

Sufis. Murat explained to father and me when I brought Raziet home to take a meal with us. She explained with translators through two different dialects so we

could barely understand the words sent from Turkic to Adyge, a language of the North Kafkas. I also spoke the Kievan dialect and some of the languages of the mountain people we lived with in the summer from my own time.

"Our enemy is common," Raziet told us.

"Don't tell me you still have the same enemy over all these years? Why do people have to have enemies?" I asked her. I'm not sure she understood where we belonged and when.

You'd be surprised at how many different faiths have leaders who say they hold direct communication with heaven, seeing their prophet, leader, or savior in the form of a dove who gives divine commands. Of all the places I traveled to and in all the times, almost everyone from everywhere sees a dove and gets divine commands from that dove. I wonder why and what that means…and why a dove? Does it mean freedom to everyone all over the world? Or does it mean peace?

Freedom and peace should be the same, but you rarely see one without the other. Some force crammed the mountaineers. The state was spreading like plague.

"We go home and wait to die because your leader thinks the Mountaineer mode of warfare is not good enough for him now," said one man at our table.

Are our faiths pre-determined to grow within us? Is war pre-destined to explode from within us no matter how many thousands of years we travel into the future? Is our past our future and our future our past? I shall travel and see for myself.

In the present, Murat came to visit the large cabin we sat in with our guests. We were the guests.

"Fighting is useless without tanks," said one warrior.

I stared out of the window watching horses clopping down the stone streets of the aoul. The streets were almost empty. Rain washed bits of colored paper from an empty market place. Flies buzzed in the sun, and doors remained bolted waiting for some word.

They showed me what a radio was, but all I heard was a blank noise. In the distance, the boom echoed across the hills. Fire and smoke and the sound of war closed in.

Therefore, the more things change, the more they change back to what they were in the first place. "What will happen to us?" I asked my new friend, Raziet.

Outside a Sufi Imam preached from a goat stand. "My words came to pass."

Inside this cabin, small tablets were placed around the room inscribed with verses.

Ornaments on the walls were weapons suspended from wooden pegs. Sabres gleamed.

The sights told me a lot about my own Khazaria. We didn't have women's rooms, but here, the rooms for females and children were separate from the others and they had no look-out windows, just shadowed lattices hiding one room from another. With no look-out windows on the passing world, no news came.

Raziet explained it wouldn't be proper for a man to question his wife or wives. Great wooden pegs and tables filled the women's rooms where they knitted their silver lace in an obscurity illumined by scanty rays of sunlight from an opening in the roof.

Raziet and her mother showed me where they live, in their own set of rooms. The walls of the women's quarters were hung with dresses and fabric, not with weapons. Yet perhaps clothes also are passive weapons.

In the corners were large boxes filled with the bedding for her house. Strung on lines across the room were embroidered napkins, scarves, silk bodices glittering with gold threads and silver flowers. The shelves were filled with copper and crass, china and glass ware, pottery, and the wooden bowls and spoons used for eating. Raziet showed me her loom.

I was offered a pottage of millet with boiled lamb and goat flesh in it. Raziet drank from leather bottles filled with sour milk and honey and some barley. I ate the wheat loaf with honey and wild thyme. Outside was a shaggy steed. In walked the Kalmyk Mongolian women who tinted their hair red with henna. We went with these women to their hut half buried in the sand on the shore.

A boy ran to meet us with a falcon on his wrist. Then we saw him—the Bavarian, General Neid. The women told us through a translator, but we understood the Tatar women. I learned a new word—the Nazis were all over the mountains. Who are the Nazis? Oh, yes. Murat told me what had happened. Then he told me about the soldiers who deserted their Nazi ranks and were hiding and creeping in the mountains. All over the mountains the men searched for deserters from the Nazi ranks.

"He was sent into the Kafkas to carry out a system of defense and conquest," they warned me. Raziet pointed to the older Tatar woman. "Murat uses German and Polish deserters to make Dargo their headquarters.

He collects stores of ammunition and provisions."

"What side is that man on?" I asked.

"We can't be too sure." The Tatar woman grinned. "He uses the zeal of the tribes all over this part of the Kafkas. He's defensive. Watch out, but he isn't making any progress in stepping on us highlanders. He's been here two years, and is losing ground."

"How do you know all this?"

The Tatar woman laughed. "I listen to the men talk. I sleep with one eye open. The men around here say he has the power of life and death over the mountain people. He'll put anyone he wants on trial for offences, and he appoints the civil workers. Someone hired him to put down us few rude tribes in the mountains."

"Who hired him?" I looked at the women. "Don't tell me you mountain men are still battling the Russians for independence after more than a thousand years. What did you expect—the Nazis to set you free? What about us steppe and mountain Jews? Whose side are you on anyway, my friends?"

"Nothing short of the capture of Dargo would kick the Germans out and restore Russian rule of the twelve tribes of the Caucasus Mountains." The Tatar whispered to me.

"Is that what you want, more Russian rule over your people?"

"We want independence," the Tatar shouted.

"Here, have a bite of this cake." She shoved her honey cakes in my mouth to shut me up. It was toasty and sweet.

I studied Neid's face from a few paces away later that day. The blackness beneath his eyes told me he wasn't eating well. What I didn't know wouldn't harm me, yet.

Murat left his meal with the mountaineer men and my father and went to see the Tatar woman's men folk.

"I have a plan," he told his followers at the Tatar's place. "With a force of ten thousand infantry and a few hundred Cossacks, I'll set out for Dargo, taking the northern track, the route by the river Koissu and through the district of Andi."

The Tatar males agreed. "The mountaineers will watch all the enemies."

"Only small parties are to show themselves. The villages will be left without police indefinitely."

Women were afraid they'd be molded by grief, but suddenly the latest infantry rifles came into the hands of the mountaineers. Their world was smelted together into a unity for an undetermined goal. If one mountaineer fed the enemy a spoon of yogurt—laban, the Russians would take their revenge on the Sufi Mountain Men.

Nazis had just exterminated thousands of Russians on the front. And they were ready for revenge on any mountaineer who thought for one instant that the Nazis would promise the mountaineers a homeland free from the Russians.

Enemies boxed in the hills from all sides. Neid, the German general who had run away from his Nazi army walked into the house of the Tatars. "You work in a factory?" He asked the woman's old husband.

"I'm a machinist," said the Tatar.

"That's the myth of the happy worker," the deserter grinned.

"And what about you?" He looked right through me.

"I'm getting married." I didn't know what else to say.

"So? If you're not in school, then you belong in the factory."

What was I going to say, that I'm a Jewish Khazarian Princess? Luckily, the Tatar man spoke up. "From whom do you get your soldier's pay?"

"What?" Neid said sharply.

"We don't depend on the fifth of the booty taken from the enemy or the fines imposed for violations of the shariat."

The Tatar moved closer to Neid. "We have a system of taxation. A poll tax to the amount of the ruble is levied on every family. One tenth of the produce of the land goes into the public treasury. If you die without heirs, your money goes to the government. And wealth is accumulated in the mosques.

"The Sufi dervishes living on voluntary contributions have been absorbed into our army or driven out of the land. Our general lives as simply as we do. The Imam is rich and deposits money in secret places in the woods of Ani and Itchkeria—great treasures of gold, diamonds, and other valuables."

As Neid scrambled to his feet the Tatar man laughed. He looked at me or through me as if I were invisible, assuming from my gaudy Khazar clothing, straight brown hair, and high cheekbones that I was a Tatar.

"Riches are a strong ally," Neid grumbled.

"But simple living makes us outlast you." The Tatar walked around him. "We number only a million and a half, maybe less now. The Russians are returning to the front by way of Transcaucasia and Cis. Better watch out, General Neid."

"Large expenditure for such a small result," the General said.

"Where do you stand? I know you're a deserter, but what side are you really on, or did they plant you here?"

"They?"

"Someone set you up in the mountains. I don't believe you're hiding out here."

"This damned Kismet of yours," Neid scowled.

"You see us through foreign eyes," the Tatar man added. "I heard there's a wedding."

"No wedding in wartime," Raziet said.

"Then what?" Neid paced the floor. "I know the trap will close on Berlin."

"Whom can we trust?" Raziet whispered to me.

"Only yourselves." I told her. "Always be prepared."

A whistle made us jump from the smoking breach in the front line. Not hands, but two would do just fine. Ahead lay a long journey, and we had no chance to return to that cave and trace our footsteps and markers placed to get back to our own homeland and time. We weren't in a hurry.

There could be a war there, too, if we didn't get the exact year we came out of. One of the Mountain Men began to sing an old song that had been around the Kafkas for centuries:

"I rejoice if I see a Khazakh, galloping on horseback and wearing the tymakh."

I told him we used a *tymakh* also, but it wasn't something we wore. It was a musical instrument we played. Then she showed what the piece of clothing looked like. So words get changed over the centuries and are used by neighboring tribes to mean different articles.

"Foreign workers!" The cry went up from the Nazis we saw. "Workers from the Caucasus." Only now we were in the West Kafkas and we had come from the East Kafkas.

Mountain men were being brought into Germany to work in large numbers as the people were shouting why are their own commanders doing that when the war was in part about expelling large amounts of people considered foreign.

The Nazi's war was about excluding, segregating, and expelling people they didn't like, and made up labels and names that these people were not as good as themselves. That was an excuse to get them out so boundaries could be established, racial, land, and political. Once boundaries were in place like neat little lists, more living space would be provided for their own people, so the line went.

That was the same line the Kievan prince used on us long before our conversion. Now, it was 1942, and the tribesmen told me that a quarter of their labor force was made up of foreign workers and those who worked by force with no pay.

The farms were "manned" by foreign workers supervised by farm women, old men, and boys. As more foreign workers, usually unpaid, were dragged into their country, the Nazi fears gave way to terror. And all along they started the whole thing by wanting to cleanse their country of foreign workers.

That was what Prince Svyatoslav wanted, or was it? Maybe he really did mean "nothing personal" as he said. Perhaps he didn't care who we are, but really only liked to fight. He'd fight anyone—us, the Pechenegs, and anyone else who appealed to him for a fight. To Svyatoslav we were a game. He had to fight someone just so he'd feel like his old self again.

There's always a type of man—or woman, like the Queen of the Steppes who had a need to wage war. It was as if he or she was so understimulated to begin with—in her mind and body, that only to bring her up to the level of well-being or normal, he or she liked to fight and had to wage combat.

The whole lot of us except my father, the Kagan, the Khatun, and my brother, stayed behind. Everyone else finally landed in one of the 22,000 camps in Germany. All the tribesmen we had camped with landed in Ohrdruf, a concentration camp for Russian and Mountain men and other minority groups.

Word got back to us that several days before the arrival of the troops of liberation. The Nazis brought out all their inmates of the camp to the square in the center of the camp and had killed them.

You can look this up for yourself, whatever time zone you're in now. It was reported by Vernon Kennedy, UNRRA Liaison Officer to the 12th Army Group in a memorandum detailing an inspection trip made from April 15 to 21, 1945. There were about 4,000 killed and 1,000 who survived this massacre, mostly people from the Kafkas or Rus.

So war is not what anyone would want to return to in any time zone. Well what happened was eerie. When it came to the Mountain men, some people had the idea that if they didn't want to return to Russia, then they must have collaborated with the Nazis.

Actually, they were afraid of being under the thumb of the communists where they were treated badly. So one group of Mountain men refused to return to Russia and began to fight the liberating troops who only wanted to pick them up and free them so they could return to Russia.

Then word got around that a few distinguished Mountaineer generals who had fought on the side of the White Russians in the old Russian Civil War had emigrated and held Austrian or German citizenship from the years before this war. These generals tried to intervene with the authorities.

They failed, and voluntarily returned with the others. As leading White "Russian" officers, automatic execution awaited these generals in Russia, but they voluntarily returned anyway. Then I heard what happened, all about the Mountaineer suicide rite, the 'adat' or unwritten law of the mountains that took hold. Their honor would not be defaced.

Well, we Khazari don't have any suicide rite of the mountains or the steppes. We have the Torah. That's what we answer to. So just after breakfast, Atokay raised a nervous fist and began to hammer on the door of the International Refugee Organization.

"Let me in, I tell you." He growled at the clerks.

"Stop that banging." The door opened a bit and Atokay put his foot in it. We stood behind him.

"War criminals, quislings, traitors!" We heard the shout go up around us.

"No, we're Jews," the Kagan answered. No one believed him in that Khazar dress until he showed the skull cap under his other mountaineer's cap.

The voices began, "Any other persons who assisted the enemy in persecuting civil populations or voluntarily assisted the enemy forces, ordinary criminals, and persons of German ethnic origins, whether German minorities in other countries, who have been transferred, evacuated, or have fled into Germany...."

"Hey, but we are Khazari, Jewish steppe peoples." Nobody believed us in this time zone.

"When they have acquired a new nationality, they become otherwise firmly established. When they have unreasonably refused to accept the proposals of the Organization for their resettlement or repatriation, or..."

The one in authority kept on reading, "When they are making no substantial effort toward earning their living when it is possible for them to do so, or when they are exploiting the assistance of the Organization."

Atokay sat next to his wife. The clerk warned him, "The main object of the Organization is to bring about a rapid and positive solution of the problem which will be just and equitable to all concerned. The main task is t encourage and assist in every way possible early return to their countries of origin. No international assistance should be given to traitors, quislings, and war criminals, and nothing should be done to prevent in any way their surrender and punishment."

Atokay confronted the International Refugee Organization officer reading his constitution and explaining it to the others. "Stalin is exterminating the Mountain Men in Russia because someone told him that a few sided with the Germans to get out from communism. Do you believe that story?"

The clerk cleared his throat. "The constitution provides for individual freedom of choice. We handle valid objections to repatriation."

A shuddering silence filled the room. Atokay watched the blue veins in his bare feet grow fat. "Persecution or fear based on grounds of persecution because of nationality provided these are not in conflict with the principles of the

United Nations as laid down," the clerk continued to speak in a flat tone.

"Objections of a political nature judged by the Organization to be valid."

"What do you mean—valid?" Atokay questioned him.

"Do you believe the entire peoples of the North Kafkas or the émigrés who fled to Austria and Germany sided with the Germans to escape Russia's treatment of mountain people and Communism?"

"What should I believe when a see a few Mountaineer generals trying to help your people, Generals who had fled to Austria and Germany who were not judged to be of such an inferior "race" as the Nazis put it, that they were promoted to generals? What should I think?" The clerk's faced blushed as he spoke to Atokay.

"We want the Kafkas to be free, that's all. We are not traitors, and we didn't fight for the Germans."

"Well, Turkey didn't exactly go with the allies either at the start of the war," the clerk answered. "We're not Turks."

"Some of the tribes of the North Caucasus do speak a Turkic language, but most speak one of the North Caucasus Mountains dialects, I know," the clerk said. "I also know you people sought independence under the protection of England and Turkey. That's the real reason Stalin killed 800,000 North Caucasus Mountains people and

sent the remainder to prisons in Kazakhstan. This I know."

"There can be no religion under Stalin." Atokay bowed his head and pounded on the clerk's desk.

"Stalin is our ally," the clerk answered defiantly.

"Are you doing this to me to save your own face for the Soviet bloc?" Atokay turned and left.

"Wait," the clerk shouted. "We have responsibility for the care of more than seven hundred thousand refugees and displaced persons. We have a problem in France to take care of."

The clerk sat back uneasily. "Do you need medical services?" His blue eyes stared at Atokay and the rest of us standing behind him. What do you need? Blankets? A place to sleep? Name it."

"I'll name it," Atokay said in a shaky voice.

"You gave people like us to the highest bidder. Why are you treating us like next-to-nothings?"

"Don't tell me you have a sense of entitlement. You're like anyone else here. We're all equal." The clerk rubbed a spot in his shirt.

"Why are you blaming me?" Atokay paced restlessly as he spoke. "Why don't you blame it on the Cossacks?"

"Blame what?"

"Being traitors."

"The Cossacks aren't traitors."

"You know what I mean," Atokay said to him, and the rest of us as he turned to face us. "How come you distribute cash grants and furnish legal assistance to the White Russians and others with Nansen passports and to the Spanish Republicans, but Mountain Men you treat like dirt?"

"Where did you learn that?" The clerk squinted at Atokay.

"From books and travels. You're not educated unless you have traveled like I have—everywhere."

Well, he hadn't traveled in time—the ultimate education. And I have. Atokay stared at the fluttering eyelids of the IRO officer. The officer poured eye drops into his eyes while the clerk shuffled papers in a file cabinet. "We're cutting costs to the bone," the IRO officer said, looking at the clerk instead of Atokay who was talking to him.

"What does that mean for me? I'm interested in being resettled. I don't want to be repatriated. Little necessities like dental treatment and washrooms are for those not facing death as a traitor in Moscow. Where shall I go? What shall I do?"

The IRO officer yawned. "Maybe you should try New York."

"Mumtaz Allah!" Atokay raised his voice an octave. "I want my people's old flag back. It was the flag of a free Kafkas, symbol of unity. Our flag of 1830 was green with three crossed arrows and twelve stars, representing the twelve tribes of the tribes and districts of the Caucasus. Long live the valley of the apple trees, our capitol."

"Is that the city of Maikop?" The officer surmised.

The clerk intervened. "You should have thought of your beautiful valley of the apple trees that before you ran over to the Germans to be liberated from them from Russia, our ally. You're always talking about the mountains, but now you want the valley of the apple trees as well? What's wrong with going back to Russia? You'll be repatriated to where you came from."

"I'm not Russian," Atokay shouted. "I'm a Mountaineer, a Moslem. Stalin wants to kill my people. Mikoyan and Molotov signed the secret orders to kill all of my people."

And what about my family that stayed in Kiev? I thought. There was a pause and then a bell.

"Calm down," the clerk sighed. "Don't act like you are going to kill yourself in front of our building. No employment is available, except with the Germans, and refugees are not required to accept such work."

"We are good men doing good," Atokay begged and pleaded. "There's no sense in bad men doing evil. The charges are false that we sided with the Germans. We just came from fighting them in the mountains. Besides, there's a deserter from the German army hiding with us and helping us. We are not helping the men he deserted."

"You ran from communism to the first road to what you thought was freedom," the IRO officer added. "I understand. When the Nazis found you, they put you in work camps as their slaves. That's how they freed you from the Russians."

Remember the Romans? I pondered. They did the same, made the mountain men slaves by freeing them from their former masters. Does everyone who promises freedom end up making the runaway a slave? It's not that work makes free.

It is creative expression that makes free, but you have to really love what you do. Then you have to convince someone to pay for it. And finally you give it away to pay taxes. I'd have to go back to a time when there were so few people in my steppes that no one paid taxes, and everyone was free. Ah, the life of the nomad compared to the settled life in my orchards. Which really is better?

"The Germans were never in the part of the Kafkas in which we live." Atokay said. "Instead, the Russians killed most of us for begging for help."

Atokay told me yesterday that the mountaineers are all fight as long as they can see mountains, but what happens when they are taken away from their mountains or when they live in the valleys? So I gathered my brother and the rest of our Khazar family and before we were shipped away to some remote place, headed toward the secret cave near the waterfall high up in the mountains, back to the door between time boundaries.

By nightfall, all of us gathered near the cave. My father came forward and addressed the rest of the Mountain men through a man who translated between the Turkic dialects and the speech of the Kafkas.

"Come back with me to a time when your people were at peace under the Khazar rule in this same place."

"Should we accept that?"

"I'm the Kagan, and I'll grant you free choice and the freedom you want for your twelve tribes of the mountains. You can have the faith you choose."

Atokay looked at his people and took a vote. They sure didn't want to be repatriated back to Russia, and they didn't want the Nazis in their homeland, not with all the slave labor and the camps for their war machine.

That was not their idea of a free Kafkas and free mountain nations.

Darkness began to creep along the valley.

"We'll go back to your Khazaria."

"I've seen the future," the Kagan told them.

"And it isn't good for Khazaria in the future, but we can find a new homeland easily in my time. There are open lands in Polin."

"No," Atokay said, shuddering. "If your Polin is the Poland of today, it's full of war and invasions. Don't take us there."

"You could always choose to live in Syria, Jordan, or anywhere else in the Middle East," I said. "When we were flung through time, we ended up walking from Khazaria to Jerusalem, and we passed through all those lands. Would you feel at home among the peoples of Jordan, Syria, or anywhere else in the Middle East?

"What about in the villages of the Holy Land? We were great healers there, since those acupuncture needles father received from a man who owed him a great favor came in handy. You'd be surprised how those needles healed people when we followed the energy lines and zones pointed out to us by that man from Cathay."

"I know the future holds someday a free land for your peoples as it does for mine," my father said.

Now we entered into a place where the reign of terror began. We rode and rode until we ended up out of the Kafkas and into the streets of Crimean towns. Nazis marched the Crimean Turks into the streets of Simferopol, as they call it now.

This used to be a place where Khazari fled after the fortress had been destroyed. I saw the Russian Army, (they called it Soviet during the War where we landed in time-reach) occupy the Crimea and watched the deportation of Crimean Turks, the Chechen, the Ingush, and Mountain men by NKVD forces sent for that purpose.

If only I could ask them all to follow me, so we can move not between planes, but between a single plane that is—time. If I move my body one way in time—or space, my mind wants to move the other way to keep the center of time where it was.

There had to be room to take the deportees with us back through the cave, but what if it became overloaded and closed up on us? We took a vote.

Our family, Atokay, all his Mountain men, and the Khazari we brought with us would go back together in time to our special place when Khazaria enjoyed a hundred years of light. Back then, the few people there danced in the streets with the joy of

learning how wisdom so old can be so new. And "then" could be "now."

It was a clear choice: Khazaria in the ninth century or New York City in 1942. On the other hand, I could have my teeth fixed better in New York. Only we made a vow.

We sent messages in many languages to the deportees and sent other messages on to the Jews in the camps or on their way, or in hiding to spread the word. We told them where the secret cave of time was located.

If only someone would believe us and look for the opening in the fabric of time deep in that cave, they could come back to the other end of that place and emerge in our time either in the Kafkas where we entered, or somewhere in Khazaria, the third branch where the cave opened in time.

There had been other branches opening in other places and times, but we didn't have the chance yet to try all the places where at certain times of the year, openings would begin to pulse in the rock, and anyone could take a leap of faith and find his destiny on the other side far in the past.

We let them know where our markers had been tied. If only someone had the chance to escape and believe us and really try to find that cave opening. When we got back to our own time, the Byzantines, who are our allies at this time, but won't be in a hundred years, might be looking for someone to blame for the attack on them by the Rus that happened right before we left to go up into the mountains far away from Atil and Sarkel.

Did the Emperor suspect the Khazari? In our time, the Dnieper trade route had not yet been built. In the next century, it was. My father gave the Rus permission to sail their fleet down the Don, past the fort of Sarkel so they could enter the Black Sea from the Don. We had trouble with both sides. And Byzantine prisoners had been held by Khazari, but these prisoners had committed crimes that would be seen as criminal acts by any group of people in the world.

The Rus took those Byzantine prisoners as part of their enormous booty. Then they dropped them off at Sarkel on their return trip. We had trouble.

Then the Khazari demanded to take the Greek prisoners into protective custody, to keep the Byzantines our allies for this short span of time. As soon as we turned Jewish, the Byzantines stopped being our allies.

All of a sudden, they started looking for somebody to blame for not being prepared to battle the Rus when attacked by them. So, they blamed the Khazari for the Rus attack, when we had no idea the Rus were going to attack our Byzantines allies.

Now the Byzantines are no longer our allies. We are alone in the world, being the only Jewish Kaganate in the world in our time.

The Rus and Pechenegs are attacking us from all sides. Yet, father calls this time we are going back to, the best and most peaceful in all of Khazaria—our golden age. I thought our golden age was in eight century Cordoba.

So as we go forth in time through our secret cave, like a magical toy shop, we keep ending up in the days when the Kagan of Khazaria first began to accept the Judaic faith and customs. So back we will go. You call this peace? With a country this peaceful, who needs war?

Deportees marched into empty cattle cars filled to overflowing, locked, and sealed. Most of the Crimean Turks we followed went to concentration camps in Sverdlosk Raion in the Urals.

Most died of the hunger and disease brought on by slave labor. A small minority fled to Turkestan. So many tribes were loaded up and deported. They were the Chechen, Ingush, Karachay, Balkars, Tatars, and Mountain men. I still say we are part of the old Greek colonies and Greek Diaspora, regardless of whether we are Jewish or Christian.

Then of course, there were millions of Jewish people who outnumbered all the tribes of the Caucasus, but the Russians did not deport Jews in huge numbers. The Nazis did. Russians deported peoples of the Caucasus, and they used the excuse to deport them that a few had been traitors, looking up to the Nazis to rescue them from the Russians.

Maybe they should have called a Khazar. That's who you call when all hope is gone, if you want a mortal, that is. As history had it, Khazari peoples had scattered and worked their way into populations of many countries and maybe disappeared by the time zone we are in now, marrying into and mingling with everyone around them until they became part of the whole patchwork of the world.

Time changes everything, but people deep down change very slowly. Time changes people less than people change time. I am fascinated about moving through time. And I'm also curious about pioneering space. In the ninth century to move through space you either travel or dance. If you want an education, travel and mingle.

As I look down from the mountains, I'm filled with a passion to run, to roll in the grass with my dogs and wolf cubs, to fight the pull of the earth ever downward. It can all be summed up as my horizontal expression of a vertical desire to grow up like a tall tree and reach out with my branches to every corner of the world.

Life cannot be contained in a small space. It's the old nomadic reach fighting against the need of the settled farmer to grow orchards and put down deep roots instead of far-reaching branches. You become the horiztonal expression of your vertical wish to move up the ladder.

The earth has become too small to reach sideways. One stretch and you've squashed your palm into the face of the person next to you. Life on the Silk Road as a nomad has become too complex.

Dear Diary, even now, I feel the closing in of compartments, the containment of life in small spaces. I, even as Princess of the Khazari, have only the personal space of my own limited to what I can carry in my pockets.

Even my room is not my own. Everything is shared, down to the last morsel of our thin, flat Khazar bread. My only privacy is in my little leather purse that I wear around my neck on a long leather thong. Even my baby cousin reaches into my pockets and pulls out a toy. At least my purse has draw strings.

So the vertical expression to build up of a horizontal desire reach out to our neighbors and the horizontal expression to reach out to the world for more land of the vertical desire to grow in wisdom up toward righteousness forms this fourcornered box. And I'm contained after all, it the box.

Let me out. I want to be free. No I want to be protected....No I want to travel through time and space. All this conflict is the reason for my adventure, my time travel, my leap of faith through space.

And only our family knows of the opening in the fabric of time. That cave, that old watery place. I must get back to the secret cave and go back to my Pax Khazarica, my own home and time.

We watched, Dear Diary, and hid in the woods. We still wore our Khazari clothing from a thousand years before this war, and in this entire ruckus, nobody noticed that these clothes were not from some isolated mountain tribe deep in the Kafkas. So we gathered our friends who did have transportation and hitched a ride back to the place we started from in the Kafkas before someone noticed our strange appearance in these time-worn clothes.

We left the Crimea, watching the cattle cars depart and make history. Not a minute too soon. We traveled for what seemed like centuries, but it was a very long drive from the Crimea back the Kafkas. We crouched and crept along the roads and into the woods.

At the right place in time and geography we met up with our Mountaineer friends. They also fled with us to escape being deported to an empty desert along the Silk Road. That's where the Rus wanted to send us in our own time, and here in the 1940s, they would have sent us there once more.

Only now there were no more great trade caravans along the Silk Road to take us up on long journeys and sell us fine acupuncture needles from Cathay so we could earn our way as miracle healers in disguise as pilgrims.

Mother came in. "I'll show you the way back to the cave and to our time. At least the rest of your own lives and your children will be in peace, in the pax Khazarica, as the Latins visiting Byzantium have called our times."

The vote sided with father. Everyone in the aoul decided to come with us back to Khazaria in the days when the Kagan's family had first turned Judaic for those who chose to take that faith.

"I promise you all freedom to live in my land and choose whatever faith you want," said father.

"We have people from almost everywhere in the known world living in our country and worshipping as he or she wants. This is the only place in our part of the world where such is the law of the Kagan of the Khazari."

We formed a human chain, hand in hand and tied a rope around each of our waists to keep together in a line. As darkness fell, we were back in the cave where I had tied my silver lace in little pieces of fabric all along the route. I knew where the road split in two and had tied a bouquet of flowers on a post to mark the route back home to my own time and place.

We trekked through the winding paths, beyond the stalagmites and stalactites. I checked each tiny piece of silver lace to keep on the trail. Finally, we came to the dark opening in the cave. There were old paintings there as we lighted a torch of twisted reeds to see our way and feel for the sharp wind and the pulse in the fabric of time at the opening of the time travel entrance.

The torchlight threw eerie shadows on the walls. Someone had painted horses and bison on those caves, and part of the cave was under water. We walked for hours until the waterline and the rock that I marked to show the opening into time began to pulse in the opposite direction from the edges where it closed when we whirled out. I took a leap of faith, and I was in first, and then my brother tied in back of me, and all the rest.

The Kagan went last, out of custom for his safety. He let us test the waters first, but I knew we would be in and out of there in a flash. So around we went, and through the maze of time. We floated and swam as if in a pond, a salty well of all beginnings. And we again where swirled through time, kicking past the great year our Khazaria's fortress at Sarkel had been destroyed and we had to flee.

We moved past that with all our might and faith, and moved and flailed until we came out the other end of the tunnel at the great blue-white light that branched into gold rivers leading to different times.

Which one was our new beginning, the first day in Khazaria that I became aware that all time is the great gold circle on the tree of life that can not be locked—that it expands forever? I chose the light.

"No, don't choose the light," Atokay shouted.

"It's a trick to get you to go there like a moth. You'll be trapped in a box forever."

"I'm choosing the light because it leads to freedom." I echoed back to him.

"Choose the dark," my brother agreed with him. It leads back to our home. You can't see, but you can feel the great mass of dark matter."

"I'm choosing the light as I chose to light the oil lamp and walk out of the dark," the Kagan told us.

"I'm going with the light because I want to see truth," Khatun said with a voice of compassion and strength. "The light is righteousness."

"The dark is righteousness. The light is a trick to lock your souls in a box forever," my brother shrieked in his changing voice. Only bugs go to the light and they get burned or trapped.

Curiosity draws the light to you, and you get killed by curiosity like a cat drawn to a trap."

"You learn by curiosity," I disagreed with my brother. "My brain is bigger than a cat's."

Khatun sighed. "I'm going to take that leap of faith and go toward the light. It worked before by accident when we were hurled into the year Khazaria fell. It will bring us back. It's the only sign we know, and let's all go to what is familiar. We must go with precedence."

"No, you go to what's familiar even when what is familiar is pain," my brother warned.

"We're all going toward the light," a chorus of voices from all the men from the Mountain men spoke together.

"The light it is. It worked before," I said. My brother reluctantly agreed. We moved toward the light, swimming and flailing, our arms pushing the thick air and underground black water like frogs in a pond.

And in an instant the pulsing light and the walls of the cave closed in and expelled us beyond all time and space through a whirlwind and faster and faster we spun like dreidles (Festival of Lights tops) on Hannukah. We were great spinning tops, and floating kites of the children of the Silk Road. We spun and spun until we were almost fabric woven into the cloth of time ourselves, this long chain of human longing. We wove ourselves through the fabric of time.

Out we leaped, rolling like boulders onto the soft summer petals. It was daylight now, early morning with the sun beginning to rise, and the mist on the meadows showed us we were reborn.

"What's that?" Khatun pointed. "Where are we?"

"It's the mighty fortress at Sarkel," my father said cheering. "It's not destroyed. It's just being prepared for the summer, and getting a good washing down at that."

"Welcome to Sarkel everyone." I said cheering.

My brother leaped for joy. We all joined hands. The Mountain men looked around getting used to the site.

"What year is this?" my father asked anyone who heard him as he walked to the door. A soldier came up to greet him and recognized him.

"My Kagan," the solider said. "Why, how did you arrive so soon in Sarkel? It was only yesterday that you gave your decision to accept the Judaic faith for the royal family. Why I heard you say that you had hoped the people would imitate the Kagan's family as so many strive to-- and also take an interest in possibly choosing the faith you selected."

"I see," said the Kagan.

"But, but…you told us you were going to spend many days traveling into the mountains to reflect at your summer residence. How did you travel back here so soon?"

"I never left because Khazaria is not only a state of mind, it's also everywhere one travels," the Kagan said.

"It's more important that we welcome our new people to the royal court. Show them the full hospitality of how those who come to live in our lands are honored and given the freedom to choose their own faith.

Let them see what Khazar tolerance and friendship is about and how much it will show them our warmth, charity, and blessings. They are now part of Khazaria and equal to anyone else who lives here."

The soldier saluted his Kagan and hurried away. Then the The Mountain men led by Atokay looked around Khazaria in awe of what life used to be not too far from their own lands.

Taklamakhan and her new husband walked up to us to continue her wedding that would go on for weeks with feasting and music. It was a time in Khazaria to begin all times. This is a day of joy and enlightenment. And this is how I will remember it always. I am Raziet-Serakh, flower of all the Turkic peoples, and my land borders the Sea of Meotis, the sea of the Khazari.

Now I have something else to add. Upon converting to the Judaic faith, I make a promise to relinquish all other faiths that I have been before adopting the faith.

How can I relinquish all that is my past generations? Who will light a candle in memory of all my peoples of all times? Yet I am part of the Silk Road and its music, joy, and soul, and I go back more years than can be written by time.

How can I forget the song of the open road? And how can I forget my responsibility to take care of the land's fruits and not use them up and move on? I can't let my goats graze recklessly and walk in the nomad's path to conquer lands anew.

And if I settle in my great orchids, can I not forget all my past and remember them as I remember Jerusalem? Who am I and where do I belong? Where are the paths to virtue and righteousness, Dear Diary?

So for this memory of a past that connects me to every other faith and to every other person, I am commanded to time travel through many lands and adventures from the beginnings of this world to its great reach into the light. And as a storyteller of tales, I am obliged to bring this story of Raziet-Serakh's adventures to all through each storyteller anew.

Go tell my tale with a truthful tongue. And speak my speech so that all may know the travels of Raziet-Serakh, princess of the Khazari, daughter of the Kagan, and one more flower from the garden of Atil or the mountains of my childhood Alania.

I am blessed by the ability to travel through time. And for that, my gifts to you are the tales for storytellers of all times and places, the adventures of the Silk Road Kids.

Stay tuned. I think as I grow up, I'm going to be more restless for travel and adventure than be suited to the life of the Khatun of the Khazari, even as a righteous ambassador of peace, healing, and enlightenment. And yes, my brother and parents travel with me. In this century, I have not yet married my dignitary from Toledo. I have moved back here, a hundred years and choose to remain not quite sixteen yet.

In fact I shall choose to stay this age a long time, and I shall choose to stay out of the century in which Khazaria is destroyed. There's plenty of time to grow up later.

I've decided that it's better to stay not quite sixteen for the energy and joy. What of my brother? He isn't unhappy at staying 13 for as long as he wants, either. It simply feels good to enjoy the best years of your life over and over again.

That's the secret of our time cave with the ancient horses and bisons painted inside where the rock opens into a new century. Now, Khazaria's in her glory years of light and abundance, and I shall think of her always this way---as my steppe sister. We have gained insight, foresight, and hindsight from this adventure. Until our next time-travel escape, I seal my *Diary*, for it is my joy toy shop.

Bihar, Kaghan of the Khazari, Marót, Raziet-Serakh, and the Khatun shall return in the next adventure to a new century in another place along the Silk Road. After all, we're steppe sisters and brothers, aren't we? Hear that, Taklamakan, Queen of the Steppes? We're steppe sisters in time. Can I buy that new horse of yours?

Thus, I write, Dear Diary:

The year Khazaria's royal family turned Jewish, I, Princess Raziet-Serakh brought the Queen of the Steppes out of her fourth century and rode with her through the tides of time along the Silk Road for the sake of righteousness. Family, friends, and I emerged through the time cave in many lands and in the middle of many wars.

My brother had to rescue the Kagan of the Khazars from captivity in the Viking ship's belly, but all turned out well back in the golden age in this common year eight hundred and sixty. Now let me look up the Hebrew year.

I could use some lessons in the many languages I am learning. This year Dear Diary, I'll stay almost sixteen. After all, my husband and child of my later years said they want to time travel at different ages before they join me next summer in real time. This story is all about being given choices to discern what is righteous, responsible, and wise for the good of all far into the great universal future. To life!

#

Stories of Values, Charity, and Virtues
The Khaz-Khan

In the earliest days of the diverse peoples that made up the Khazari and of their friends in neighboring Alania, of the Sarmatian steppes where the Volga meets the Caspian (the Sea of Meotis) and of the ancient Romans, once the mouth of the statue of the great tamga of the horse was opened. And when the mouth of the stature opened, poems could push blades of grass through the grain fields. And suddenly, there could no longer be tamga or idol, but only a gift of Hashem, the one who is wise.

In those days, a royal Mau kitten sniffed eagerly as a ramekin of chopped livers passed under his nose without stopping. An Egyptian Jewish tributary presented the twelve-week old kitten on a gold-fringed pillow. The tributary brought a Babylonian Talmud scroll in Aramaic that he inherited from his rabbi in Baghdad who tutored a family planning a coming-of-age celebration in Alexandria.

The Khazarian king, the grand Kagan, listened to the thong sandals of the children of Khans and Khaz-Khans slapping the marble floors. All watched the king unveiling the hooded cloaks of the visiting dignitaries with the gold hook at the big toes. The kitten watched the king scratch. "I shall name him after Sarkel," The king sniffed the animal's shiny coat, and the kitten sniffed back, like a tiny lion, gazing into the king's golden eyes with golden cat eyes.

Another feline extended a long pink tongue to clean her kitten's ear as the king's elbow accidentally tipped over his platter of mutton in the cat community's path. "Go protect the grain our visitors brought," he yowled. A hand waved the sniffing cats away. One velvety cat's nose leather extended broadly to sniff another's tail. With a clang of the royal gong, the cats scattered from the god-house. Then the pet wolves entered bedecked with golden harnesses so that the horse could be rubbed for good luck. All this went away when the Kagan lit the Sabbath lights and walked forever out of the darkness. But back in those earliest days, torchlight warmed the cave of the howling wolves.

By dripping torchlight that flickered against the silence of the dark long ago, in the snow and pine forests of Kiev and in Karelia, as also in the land of the Bulgars, Balkars, Karachay, Alani and Tatars, and in the lands of the Persians and the Turanians, Bulan, shepherd king of Khazaria, crossed the Caucasus and became the ancestor of the Great Bulan, then fashioned runes and the statue himself in the special divine craftsman's house.

Before the king, the floor rippled with stripes of shadow. Two priestesses shattered the torchlight within the shrine house into motion by waving fans that appeared to arch and stretch.

Bulan, one of several kings named Bulan throughout the ages, leaned forward seeking to span a more distant arc. His eyelids fluttered. He swayed to the deep voices of the priests as they uttered one, long note on the syllable, for mountain. Suddenly, he heard a faint hissing that appeared to rise from behind the enormous obsidian eyes of a visiting dignitary's personal statue-god.

"We don't have carved idols of our own. We have these," said the king. He pointed his walking stick to a totem pole decked with horse tails, tassels, silver mirrors, and Tengri-worshipped talismans. "Our people didn't carry statues along the Silk Road," Bulan said cheerfully. "Behold our fine orchards and homes. Do you see us living in yurts and leather-covered wagons?"

"Yet you do bring out a white horse for Tengri, for extra luck," said the Assyrian visitor from Mosul. We know you have been settled here for many generations," said the Assyrian dignitary wearing the cross of the Chaldean church.

"I am but one of three, a Christian, a Moslem, and a Jew. Which one will you choose as your faith and the faith of your people and those ruled by you? When will you announce your decision? Which one of us will you choose to convert you?"

I've told everyone that rabbi Ha-Sangari will convert everyone in Khazaria and under our rule who wants to be converted, but the people must choose. We have many here in the lands of Khazaria, and they come from your land as well as many other lands.

That is why they will choose, but for me, I will choose for myself and those who live in Khazaria one faith and those who want to join it will be converted with me. The king and court will take one of the three faiths.

"What will you decide?"

"I must be convinced. Since both the Christian and Moslem religions come from the Jewish religion, it must be the oldest faith in one creator. The books of all three contain names and places that come from the oldest book.

Therefore, I will convert to the oldest religion in which the others are rooted. I will join the tree at its source rather than hang from the branches and shift with the winds. After all, it's a decision based on whether to imitate successful giants of the past or make a visionary leap into changing and stormy waters."

"First we must carve the last totem pole. Or who else will light a lamp in memory of our ancestors? Something must stand in their memory and at the same time symbolize a new beginning." The young king ordered the carvers to work with him on the totem.

The king heard a noise from his totem pole as the wind made music from the charms dangling along each notch. At once recognized the loud voice he heard clearly as if from a bird perched behind his ears. Its cold command left no space to think between the hearing and the act. He had to obey.

"Carve the last totem pole this high," the visitor's voice dictated. He followed every measurement with perfection, as the figurine seemed to tell him.

"Hear my words," he carved at the base of the statue. The statue's voice seemed to come from behind the eyes. It told him how to create it.

Bulan slipped the wood deftly under his obsidian knife, reeling with the voice he heard, and then a chorus of voices, and finally the eternal chanting of the sheep sheerer in the fragrant blackness.

He stood in the shrine room of the great god-houses, the holiest city in ancient Khazaria. Bulan gazed out at his god's enormous eyes and squinted as if blinded by the sunburst of light. He pushed beads of malachite across the statue's beetling brows that rose in high relief against the torchlight.

The shafts of incense smoke quivered, sweetening the warm air with myrrh. Finally, the young king took a deep breath and ran his fingers across his head. "Remember what the ancients from far away gave us. Their lands still grow the Tree of Life. Let an ancient sound begin with the opening of the mouth ritual. I shall take up my scepter."

The tall, pale-faced king with red-gold curls parted in the center stared ahead. His eyes blazed like a topaz sunburst. Bulan fixed his gaze on the face of his personal god that arched and receded by the torchlight. As the full moon rose to its zenith overhead, the procession began with Bulan plucking the 12-stringed harp, a gift from the Assyrian visitor to his city of Sarkel.

The flat, high whistle of a reed flute melted into nuances of delight as the goat-skinned drums beat out a one, two, one two three, march.

He began the daily ritual of the temple by washing, dressing, and feeding the statues. As two attendant priests sprinkled pure water, a young and beautiful weaver of the beech forests enrobed the figure in golden-fringed garments layered in sheepskin ruffles from the shoulder to the feet of the wooden statue.

In front of the god were tables on which Bulan placed flowers and then, as a shepherd king, the flesh of sheep, bulls, goats, deer, fish, and poultry.

The first young weaver brought date wine bread and honey cakes topped with roasted figs. The hundred-priest-long line of food undulated on a bier carried above their heads. Then the priestesses and priests abandoned the statue-god to enjoy the meal alone.

Bulan retreated through a side door in the structure and went into the shrine room followed by the weavers. Then, after the moon traveled its path across an arc of sky, Bulan returned unseen, sniffed with disdain, and ate what the gods had left.

He watched the eyes of the statue as he stuffed himself with food. He was alone, and the torches were giving their last dying sparks when a young priestess entered the shrine room.

She moved swiftly through the side door to the shrine house, and seeing Bulan alone eating before the god whispered, "I see you're keeping your god in good temper."

"If you wonder whether I'm appeasing the liver of the gods," Bulan said hoarsely, "it's only at the expense of my own liver." He swallowed the last handful of sheep's flesh and reclined against the tables.

"I'm Sarai," the weaver smiled. "We came to Atil from Persia when I was a child." She brought more offerings of butter, fat, honey, and sweetmeats and placed them beside the food still overflowing on the table before the statue-god.

An angry voice resounded in Sarai's head, admonishing her. She stopped a minute to listen to her vision which she heard and not yet seen. Then a sunburst of light appeared before her eyes as if emanating from the statue's eyes. She listened and waited, and with her hand extended, reached out to touch the light. The voice was condemnatory. She immediately obeyed its cold command.

"Throw yourself at the feet of the king and beg his forgiveness, for the king is your personal god." She repeated the words.

"I'm a shepherd, not a god," he answered. Rise woman. Can you not face your god eye to eye as an equal?"

Sarai hurried from the shrine room, leaving Bulan behind the table overflowing with food and offerings. A priest returned to see what the god had eaten only to see Bulan finishing off the morsels.

"Let the opening of the mouth begin," he announced to the priest. "And find Raziet-Serakh, that wise crone who dwells in the mountains--the mother of Tamara, whose son is a great Rabbi in Byzantium. Only she can make the silent Tengri speak again as one through the voice of a twelve-stringed harp."

"Find her at once," Bulan cried. "Find my exceedingly wise commander, princess of all the great gods, exalted speaker, whose utterance is unrivaled. Summon Raziet-Serakh now!" The priest clutched his figurine and obeyed his king with the promptness that he obeyed his personal god. Bulan leapt up and hurried into the blackness of the warm night.

The line of priests to the olden gods marched first, then the high priestesses of the goddesses, walked behind. The girls' fringed cloaks shivered in the hot wind that swept up from the sea of the Khazar's edge. The sheer, transparent linen of their tunics clung to their skin, bejeweled with beads of malachite.

They oiled their tightly curled dark brown hair until it shined black and drew the coils under gold bands in braided buns. The priestesses painted their pale gold skin with lime to appear even more like alabaster. They brushed yellow ochre on their cheeks, lips, and nails.

The women stared ahead with eyes of shimmering silver that glowed transparent in the torchlight, or doe-eyes of honey, pale green, or ebony. The wife of the Assyrian dignitary showed the women of Khazaria how to draw black lines of kohl across their brows connecting them across their foreheads like bat's wings in the style of ancient dwellers of the Zagros Mountains far away in the land of the Chaldeans.

"Let the washing of the mouth ceremony begin," a priest announced as he led the procession. The king left the shrine room and stepped into the courtyard beside the house of worship his people began to build.

The king gave a hand signal summoning Raziet-Serakh, a wise old priestess. She proceeded behind him to the river's edge. Behind her, four priests carried a bier on which stood the wooden statue of the king's personal rune stone. The carving with its face of inlaid jewels rocked back and forth as the priests strained to hoist the heavy weight along the path by dripping torchlight against emblazoned runes.

At last, Raziet-Serakh stood facing the totem pole eye to eye as an equal. She did not know to kneel or grovel in the face of Tengri or in the presence of the steward-king who was a shepherd.

Imbedded in ceremonies and incantation, Bulan plunged his hand into a gold vessel filled with holy water scooped from a stream from the mountains. He washed the totem pole's wooden mouth seven times as the priests faced the statue east, west, north, and then south.

Raziet-Serakh, called the wise old lady of the steppe and mountains by Bulan, sprinkled holy water and rubbed frantically at the statue's mouth to make it speak. The priests shook the statue, pounded at its mouth, rubbed its inside with a solution of tamarisks, reeds, sulphur, gums, salts, oil of pomegranate that came all the way from Persia, and honey mixed with precious stones.

A hissing sound arose, but the god's speech was dim and too distant to be understood. Bulan wailed more incantations. The priests sounded the drums and reed flutes.

The priestesses danced, flung their fringed cloaks, unwound their sashes of indigo and scarlet, and sank back into nuances of delight, but still the face on the totem pole did not speak loudly enough to be understood by the king.

Bulan gave his own incantation, and then summoned Raziet-Serakh, the oracle. He led a smaller totem pole by the hand back into the street as the priest bellowed, "Foot that advances, foot that advances..."

Bulan stopped at the gate of the house of worship built by the newcomers and looked to the heavens. The priest, followed by Raziet-Serakh, took the hand of the god and led the statue into its own golden throne in a niche. Two priests set up a golden canopy, and Bulan, again washed the mouth of the face carved by his masters on both the small and stationary totem pole.

Raziet-Serakh stepped behind the king as the torchlight threw her high cheekbones into bold relief. She narrowed her eyes to slits and spoke in trance. "I will make that wooden plug speak." Her fingers snapped in rhythm to the drums pounding against the silence of the shrine room. "I will approach my personal god," said Raziet-Serakh. "The god which only I can hear will summon, guide of the heavens."

"The gods have abandoned us," a priestess shouted from the crowd. "Call a rabbi from Byzantium."

"Or from Persia."

"And the Crimea."

"A rabbi will make the voices be heard again."

Bulan whirled around, startled. He rested his large hand on Raziet-Serakh's bare shoulder.

"Wise old woman of Byzantium," Bulan commanded. "What tale of Talmud will you tell us tonight?"

"A tale that will close the mouth of that god you just carved and open the mouth of the one God if you learn to read the book I have brought you." The crone's eyes rolled up so only the whites showed, red veined and dirty. "I know of a rabbi in Toledo who would come here with Torah and Talmud. Then the only mouth that would be opened would be your own to the people." Bulan took a sudden interest. "I want only the oldest religion."

"The rabbi's religion is old."

"And will it give us structure that reason cannot defeat?"

"Test it against the wisest."

She soon fell into trance at the sound of Bulan 's harp notes and began to speak first in tongues and then in a singsong rhyme. As the torchlight bathed her face in eerie shadows, her voice rang out as if the leader of a chorus in the oldest and purest Khazarian dialect. It was not overgrown with the many words from the kingdom that now rose by the sea and began to change the language of Khazaria.

"It is like in the olden days with the olden gods," Bulan sighed. "Woman, what tale, I say? You try my patience with your many words."

Her rhyme grew more rhythmic as she sang to Bulan's harp in oral poem. "I shall speak of the first king of Khazaria, of a new king I shall call Obadiah the first and his God, and of the man who changed his own alphabet, and of the woman who gave him the writing for a kingdom. He took it to the entire world.

"Name this king," Bulan called out.

"This newness began before Obadiah, or the first king of Larsa, far down the river of the rabbi from Nineveh, who said no more, is the king is my god, sharru-ili, but the Torah." The woman sang in rhyme to the twang of the twelve-stringed harp.

"Show me where he is on the downward curves of the Tree of Life," Bulan commanded. Raziet-Serakh saw in the mist a great yellow light that spread out into a gold bush. In it she had a vision of Bulan as her personal god. Then she burst into song as her king as a god spoke to her. She heard Bulan 's voice as if it were a bird perched behind her ear.

Raziet-Serakh raised her bony hands and threw her silver-hair back. She sang in rapid-fire rhyming every other line exactly as her personal vision dictated to her, word for word. "My kagan, rabbi Ha-Sangari has arrived to convert the Khazars to the faith of all the Jews. Shall I tell the representatives from Christendom and Islam your decision now or after dinner?"

The Kagan smiled with the kindest of eyes. "Tell all of them that my decision will change the fate of the people of Khazaria forever. Show me what other faith inspired all three of these great religions?" I looked at my two Persian lady cats. "There's some secret in the way they sense what we cannot hear," I replied with an attitude. The Kagan arched one eyebrow michieviously, and my cats purred and in a friendly way, walked with their tails up. The cherished animals were so proud in front of all the people.

The First Kagan of Khazaria
The King Who Changed His Alphabet
Obadiah, the first king of Khazaria, stood on the virgin soil at Itil in what is today, Daghestan. For a long while he watched the distant field as

farmers with covered heads and dark red beards threshed the moist stalks with stone sickles.

He heard them singing. And he began to sing with them as he drove his sheep forward into the lush green until they reached a branch of the long river.

Obadiah was twenty and thought about how he was to choose a bride before the full moon signaled the harvest. The steward king climbed the tower as the salmon sky faded.

From the highest point he watched a young cheese maker sheering sheep. She waded in the stream until the darkness of night covered the stones where she stood feeling the white water rush over her freckled, pale gold skin.

The young king watched the moon move across the sky and the stars slowly circle toward the mountains. In the east, the peaks of the mountains like two barren horns faded, white-capped and misted in the land of the Khazari.

Obadiah, who had come to the lands of the Khazari from the Crimean shores, marked a grid with lines, plotted the path of the stars and planets and the times of plantings. He stared into the stars, trying to see a form in them and looked down again at his wet clay tablet with three scratches for every full moon, above circles for every crop planted before the moon would cycle again.

In the blackness below, the faint flicker of torchlight grew larger. He looked down from his tower as the priestess moved slowly up the stairs of the tower.

"Have you chosen your bride, yet, Obadiah?" The young king swirled around, surprised and bemused at the fourteen-year-old girl standing at the entrance to the room where he watched the heavens.

Her sheepskin tunic fell in rows of wool fringes below her hips. She wore only a necklace of lapis stones above which she twirled nervously as she spoke.

"Lady of life, Obadiah addressed the priestess, "Would you no longer serve your goddess if you were the one I choose as my bride?"

"Can we not both serve the youngest god in the heavens, as well as my goddess?" She dipped her finger in the wet clay and drew the sign of the 'cutter,' the tool used to cut the umbilical cord.

Obadiah stared for a moment at the fine-lined drawing of a cutting tool she had scratched in the clay. He looked out at the stars and then back at the four straight lines that made a picture of the cutter.

"Can we not both hear the words of great writing?" She repeated. Blood fired from her voice. Obadiah cringed at what he saw.

Obadiah had a vision and heard the voice of his god, commanding him to write down all the words for his stars and planets he had watched since he was a child.

He picked up a sliver of bone and scratched the wet clay. At first he drew two lines at angles and then one straight line down the middle.

"This is woman," he laughed. Nana slowly walked over and looked in the wet clay. "Woman?" She saw what he had drawn and blushed to her toes.

"You will be my bride," Obadiah shouted. He raised his hands and closed his eyes. As she moved toward him, he rushed past her down the stairs and ran through the wheat fields to the god house.

The same weaver broke Raziet-Serakh's trance as she shouted once more, "The gods have abandoned us."

"No!" the crone snapped, hushing her with a circular motion of her extended arm. "We have abandoned them for one God."

Bulan reflected for a moment. "The territory of our gods has changed when the king swept away our borders."

"That's why the gods no longer speak," Raziet-Serakh wailed hoarsely.

"They do speak," Bulan insisted. "We no longer hear them. We won't hear them again until I restore Itil and Sarkel as the great centers of medicine and healing and the gods are one Almighty, the wise."

"When will that be?" Raziet-Serakh turned to the crowd.

Bulan rose. "When a woman sits eye-to-eye with you again on the throne as your personal goddess... Raziet-Serakh must reign once more as the lady of the mountain people. There is famine in the steppes."

"Nana! Queen of heaven, speak now!" Raziet-Serakh sighed.

Bulan kissed the hem of the crone's cloak. "Continue your song, wise woman of the mountain. I must know how and where writing first sprang from the olden gods."

Raziet-Serakh listened to the loud voice rushing in the spring's torrent and repeated the epic rhyme in perfect hexameter until dawn. The voice thundered only to her. "There is one God, says the Torah. Here, Bulan. Read the Talmud."

"I cannot yet read that alphabet."

"Then my son, the great rabbi of Byzantium will read it to you."

"Yes, teach me. Bring him and his people here, and we will all listen to the one voice pounding against the silence of the dark. A great light has shone through the leaves."

The kitten crawled up the hem of the King's cloak and sat happily purring in his lap as the smiling king circled his fingers gently around the orange tabby's ears and offered a kiss and a blessing to all the diverse peoples of the Caucasus.

Concept/Storyline

There may not have been any concept of Bar or Bat Mitzvah in 10th century Kiev or in the rural areas of the steppes or in the isolated villages or aouls of the Caucasus Mountains 'yet,' but that wouldn't stop the nearly grown children from diverse backgrounds of Karachay-Balkaria and from Alania, the children adopted by the Kagan of the Khazari from arranging the appropriate rite of passage and blessing for the changing of the societies around them which they knew—the pagan Vikings, Rus, and Pechenegs surrounding Kiev, the Volga Finnic peoples of the Urals, the eternal Silk Road, Christian Byzantium to the south, the many and diverse mountaineers of the Caucasus, the grassland steppes, the rabbi-scholars and Christian scholars of Constantinople and Spain, the Turks arriving from Central Asia, and the Islamic Caliphate of Persia and Baghdad to the East. Each magnificent encounter began a new concept and framework for their time-travel adventures.

The garden of the Khazari and the Alani, the Karachaians and the Balkarians is a storyteller's paradise, especially during the time that the Khazari ruler's family, friends, and associates turned Jewish, and the Kagan of the Khazari got tied up in the belly of a Viking Ship, rescued by his thirteen-year-old son, and his daughter, the teenage, time-traveling Princess Raziet-Serakh.

Raziet-Serakh rode between the fourth and tenth centuries with the Queen of the Steppes. Then the family emerges during World War Two in the Caucasus. Welcome to anthropology through fiction and my time- travel novel for all *storytellers* on tales of the Silk Road Kids, and Stories of Medieval Khazaria and their friends and allies in the Caucasus.

Let my first person novel, although fiction, guide you through the walkways of anthropology and ethnology in my "Kagan's Kids of Khazaria" Time-Travel Adventures, the book for thirteen to sixteen-year old readers and also for their parents of any background. As an author of multicultural and multiethnic novels about diverse peoples that reveal friendship stories and the nuances of anthropology through fiction—stories, novels, and plays—let this novel and the treat that follows be your mentor to open doors to new opportunities, choices, roads, and destinations.

The purpose of writing these stories and novels is to reveal the back story of youth finding a voice of resilience and confidence. The various types of fiction focus on history, anthropology, the customs, taboos, hand signs, stories and folk tales through the ages reveal a common archetype that runs through each person in any location. It's the vision to find the greatest of human virtues.

This novel is a springboard, a magical toyshop, an open door to explore your own anthropology through fiction. The way to find the mainstream is through clues and patterns. You see patterns in everything and bring together two different objects or people to arrive at a completely different third object or person. It's called growth.

This collection of stories looks at Medieval Khazaria in the 9th and 10th century through the eyes of a 13-year old boy, a 15-year old girl, and their royal family of the Kagan of the Khazars. When the Kagan of the Khazars is captured and held in a Viking ship, his son must rescue him alone and help the family to walk from Khazaria to a new homeland. The boy and his father, masters of a thousand disguises must find a way to reach their destination as the boy travels with the Kagan of the Khazars, his Khatun (the Queen), and his 15-year-old sister, Raziet-Serakh.

The other stories are about a gift of a cat in medieval times in the area between the Black Sea and the Caspian Sea followed by another tale of time-travelers.

In the 9th century, fifteen-year-old Princess Raziet-Serakh, rides with the eighteen-year old Queen of the Steppes and acts as the Queen's confident and friend.

They time-travel with the Kagan's family and the Khatun (Queen of the Khazars) visiting many lands in the Caucasus and in the Steppes of Medieval Eurasia. Their time-traveling takes them as far away as walking to Jerusalem in disguise or emerging from the imaginative time-traveling Weasel Cave in the middle of World War II in the Caucasus, when they must find their way back home to 9th century Khazaria and the Caucasus when those lands were in their glory and golden ages.

The Silk Road Kids are back on the steppes of Eurasia from the Caucasus Mountains to Kiev, from the Black Sea to the Caspian Sea, and the valleys and grasslands that reach out between all these points. The family time travels in the days when some of the empire of the Khazars, such as the royal family, and their diversified subjects, accepted the Judaic faith.

The 9th century Khazar Empire controlled the lands situation between the Black Sea (Sea of Pontus) and the Caspian Sea, (Sea of Meotis) also known as the Sea of the Khazars. Medieval Khazaria reigned from the area where the Volga

River flows into the Caspian and along the Don River. Trade routes branched out from Kiev.

The timetraveling royal family of the Kagan of the Khazars, his teenage children and the Khatun (Queen) take their family, friends, and allies on a time-traveling journey, including riding with the Queen of the Steppes and the Mountain Men of the Caucasus. Through tides of time their message pounds against the silence of the dark.

The Silk Road Kids' Adventures in history is a series of novels for young adults and all ages that follows one family, the royal family of the medieval Khazars through their secret cave in the Caucasus through which they are able to travel through time and arrive in different or the same places, but in a variety of centuries.

They bring with them those who wish to join them, the war-weary, the tired, and the people seeking a new homeland and rest. Open the doorway to the secret cave of time-travel adventure in the lands of silks and spices, tamgas and talismans, horses and mountains, steppes, and trilling drums.

Through the secret cave, they left their own war-torn Khazaria in 965 only to emerge in the Caucasus in the middle of World War II. How would they get back to their scented gardens and summer palace? And in the garb of pilgrims, the family of a thousand disguises walks from the Caspian Sea to Jerusalem to take on the life of healers with Silk Road acupuncture needles, and eventually returns to their Khazaria in its 9th century glory days when their duty was to rescue their oppressed allies in many lands.

When out of the fourth century and into the tenth, the Queen of the Steppes insists upon finding a husband and picks the wrong one, it's time to time travel again to another century and location along the ancient Silk Road. The wandering stars of Atil are on yet another adventure through time and distance. This is a novel of friendship for all peoples, everywhere.

#

Appendix

Available Paperback Books Written by Anne Hart

Browse Each Book at the Publisher's Web site at http://www.iuniverse.com. Click on Bookstore. Books also are listed with most online booksellers. Author's Web site is at http://annehart.tripod.com.

1. 101+ Practical Ways to Raise Funds: A Step-by-Step Guide with Answers
2. 101 Ways to Find Six-Figure Medical or Popular Ghostwriting Jobs & Clients
3. **102 Ways to Apply Career Training in Family History/Genealogy**
4. 1700 Ways to Earn Free Book Publicity
5. 30+ Brain-Exercising Creativity Coach Businesses to Open
6. 32 Podcasting & Other Businesses to Open Showing People How to Cut Expenses
7. 35 Video Podcasting Careers and Businesses to Start
8. 801 Action Verbs for Communicators
9. A Perfect Mitzvah Gift Book
10. A Private Eye Called Mama Africa
11. Ancient and Medieval Teenage Diaries
12. Anne Joan Levine, Private Eye

toothpaste, shampoo, and pesticides from zinc, plants, calcium, oils, or vitamins. Shine hardwood floors and furniture with tea and linseed oil. Here are the best of the recipes and also where to find more home-made cleaning or greening recipes on-line.

87. How Nutrigenomics Fights Childhood Type-2 Diabetes & Weight Issues: Validating Holistic Nutrition in Plain Language. ISBN: 0-595-53535-6.

88. Traveling Poems and Short Stories. Published both in paperback and as an e-book by lulu.com. See: http://www.lulu.com/content/3879306.

#